Once she got rid of Riley she'd be safe. Wouldn't she?

His hand dropped to her shoulder, and she twisted her head around. He slid his fingers up to her throat, his eyes now a dark blue clouding over like a stormy sea. Her pulse ticked wildly beneath his touch.

"Be careful, beach girl." Then he cupped the back of her head and drew her close, sealing his lips over hers.

The quick kiss didn't feel like goodbye. It felt like a protective stamp that she'd carry with her forever.

She managed an inarticulate goodbye as she scrambled out of the car. Walking toward the police station, she didn't dare turn around even though she could feel Riley's gaze searing her back.

She hoped the police could help her even though she didn't trust them. She hoped for once they could reassure her and make her feel safe.

As safe as she felt with Riley.

CAROL ERICSON

NAVY SEAL SECURITY

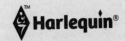

TORONTO NEW YORK LONDON
AMSTERDAM PARIS SYDNEY HAMBURG
STOCKHOLM ATHENS TOKYO MILAN MADRID
PRAGUE WARSAW BUDAPEST AUCKLAND

To K.F. and L.F., the best Los Angeles County
Junior Lifeguards on the beach.

Recycling programs
for this product may
not exist in your area.

ISBN-13: 978-0-373-69534-8

NAVY SEAL SECURITY

Copyright © 2011 by Carol Ericson

This edition published by arrangement with Harlequin Books S.A.

For questions and comments about the quality of this book please contact us at Customer_eCare@Harlequin.ca.

www.eHarlequin.com

Printed in U.S.A.

ABOUT THE AUTHOR

Carol Ericson lives with her husband and two sons in Southern California, home of state-of-the-art cosmetic surgery, wild freeway chases, palm trees bending in the Santa Ana winds and a million amazing stories. These stories, along with hordes of virile men and feisty women, clamor for release from Carol's head. It makes for some interesting headaches until she sets them free to fulfill their destinies and her readers' fantasies. To find out more about Carol, her books and her strange headaches, please visit her website at www.carolericson.com, "where romance flirts with danger."

Books by Carol Ericson

HARLEQUIN INTRIGUE

*Brothers in Arms

Don't miss any of our special offers. Write to us at the following address for information on our newest releases.

Harlequin Reader Service
U.S.: 3010 Walden Ave., P.O. Box 1325, Buffalo, NY 14269
Canadian: P.O. Box 609, Fort Erie, Ont. L2A 5X3

CAST OF CHARACTERS

Amy Prescott—A San Diego County Lifeguard, Amy gets embroiled in a drugs-for-arms deal that brings her past crashing down around her. Can the sexy Navy SEAL who comes to her rescue keep her safe or will falling for him torpedo her well-ordered world?

Riley Hammond—A former member of the covert ops team, Prospero, Riley has a single-minded mission: locate missing Prospero member Jack Coburn. However, when his mission lands him on the beach of a lifeguard with plenty to hide, he's not sure whether to interrogate her or take her in his arms.

Carlos Castillo—The ex-boyfriend Amy dumps when she finds out he's married, but Amy soon discovers Carlos has a lot more to hide than a wife.

Ethan Prescott—Amy's half brother is the heir apparent to their father's criminal enterprise. Although Amy hasn't seen him in years, he knows all about her and is willing to jeopardize her safety for his own means.

Eli Prescott—Amy's father sits in prison a broken man, but do his connections and influence extend beyond the bars of his cell?

Farouk—Prospero's former nemesis has expanded his business model and taken his terror worldwide, and this time it's personal.

Colonel Scripps—Prospero's coordinator, the colonel knows he can summon all of the former team members with one call. He just hopes it's not too late to save Prospero's leader, Jack Coburn.

Jack Coburn—The former leader of Prospero and current hostage negotiator has run into a little trouble. Can he depend on his brothers in arms to save him, or is he going to have to save himself?

Prologue

Jack Coburn could think of about a thousand tastes more pleasant than his own blood—so he spit it out. The behemoth facing him sneered and readied his ham-hock fists for another round of punch-the-stupid-American. Lurch had to be the biggest Afghan Jack had ever seen in his life, and he'd seen plenty.

Jack hadn't escaped his captivity from a small, airless tent to be thwarted here. He dug his boots into the dirt outside the cave and tensed his muscles. If he could take care of Lurch and drag his body into the scrubby bushes that clung to the side of the mountain, he could get back to eavesdropping on the conversation in the cave.

And if he'd correctly heard the name they'd dropped in there just before Lurch materialized, he had to listen in on the rest of that discussion. His life depended on it, as did the lives of his brothers in arms—the whole gang from Prospero.

Lurch charged forward, and Jack met his assault with a kick to the substantial gut. Lurch staggered back, emitting a guttural cry from his throat. The howl unleashed several pairs of footsteps from the front of the cave, and Jack spun around to meet his adversaries.

The Afghans gathered in a semicircle around Jack

and, as he waited for the gunshots, a muscle ticking wildly in his jaw, he whispered, "Bring it on."

The men closed in on him and the stench of their sweat permeated his nostrils. Or was it his own sweat?

Still, not one of the fierce mujahideen raised a weapon. Licking his lips, Jack took two steps back to the edge of the cliff and glanced over his shoulder at the outcroppings that dotted the long way down to the village where he'd been staying. Would his young friend, Yasir, be looking for him?

The leader of the group brandished his sword. He growled in the Darwazi dialect, "Who are you? What are you doing here?"

Jack pretended not to understand the man's words. He spread his hands and smiled, nodding like a fool and taking another step toward the precipice.

Even if they believed him to be harmless, they'd never let him live. And once they compared notes with their brethren, the men who'd captured him two days ago, they'd torture him for information.

If he had to die sooner rather than later, he'd prefer to die swiftly and while in control of his own destiny.

So he stepped off the ledge and into the dark abyss. Before he hit the vicious rocks below, one thought pierced his brain.

Sorry I failed you, Lola. Whoever you are.

Chapter One

A dark shape bobbed on the water outlined by a muted orange sunset and then disappeared. A seal? Amy squinted at the horizon, spotting another object in the fog-shrouded distance. That one had to be a boat.

She leaned the flag in the corner of the lifeguard tower and grabbed a broom. After sweeping the sand out the door, she dumped the hot water from the bucket onto the beach. They kept the hot water available in the tower to treat stingray stings, but with the kids back in school and the summer crowds gone, they didn't really need it. She liked to follow the rules in case anyone challenged her. She didn't need trouble. She'd had enough.

She lifted the receiver of the red phone and called the main lifeguard station up the coast. Zeke Shepherd picked up on the first ring.

"This is Amy Prescott in Tower Twenty-eight. I'm out of here."

"Hey, Amy. Catch any excitement on your last day?"

"Not unless you count an older couple out for a walk with their metal detectors and a couple of joggers. This fog is starting to roll in pretty fast. It drove everyone away about a half hour ago."

Zeke snorted. "I hate Tower Twenty-eight once the

summer's over. No people, no action. Do you want me to pick you up in the truck and give you a ride back to your car?"

"No, thanks. I'm jogging back."

"You're in such good shape you should've kicked that guy's butt when you found out—"

Amy cut him off. "See you later, Zeke."

Had every lifeguard in San Diego County heard she'd been duped by a married man a couple months ago?

She slammed the receiver back in its cradle. She might as well have Gullible Sap tattooed on her forehead. For all the precautions she usually took with relationships, Carlos had really played her.

Reaching up to unlatch the cover of the lookout window to swing it down, she glanced at the ocean. The animal on the water had moved closer to shore and now looked bigger than a seal. Amy snagged the binoculars from the hook and turned them toward the object.

A breath hitched in her throat. Two scuba divers had broken the surface and seemed to be struggling toward the beach. Had one of them lost air? Embolized?

Amy shimmied out of her sweat pants, yanked the sweatshirt over her head and dropped them both on top of her open backpack. With her heart racing, she lifted the phone off the hook and left it dangling. Of course, she'd already told Zeke she was leaving, but protocol prevailed. If someone did call the tower, the busy signal would indicate a rescue.

Grabbing her orange rescue can, she sprinted down the ramp of the lifeguard tower and churned up dry sand on her way to the ocean.

The divers, still struggling, had moved closer to the shoreline. Amy high-stepped over the waves and plunged into the chilly water, dolphin-kicking her way to the two people.

One diver had his arm around the other diver's neck, the man flailing in his grasp. *That technique would kill him, not rescue him.*

Amy shouted as she neared the duo, and the stronger diver looked up. The person in his arms slumped and he released him into the water. Adrenaline pumped through Amy's system as she shot forward and caught the disabled diver before the next wave rolled in, dragging him back out to sea.

She hooked one arm around his chest while offering the rescue can to the other diver. He shook his head and plowed through the water toward the beach with a strong stroke.

He seemed to have a lot of strength left; why hadn't he helped his buddy? He might be disoriented or in shock. She'd call the station as soon as she got this one to shore and revived him.

Still clutching the unconscious diver, Amy rode the last wave onto the wet sand. The other diver had reached the beach ahead of her and now struggled out of his gear, dropping his tank to the ground.

Rolling the victim onto his back, Amy called out to the other man. "Are you okay?"

He ripped his mask from his face and tossed it onto the sand. "Don't bother. He's dead."

His cold words felt like another splash of ocean water on her face. Then she took in his heaving chest and a jagged rip along the side of his wet suit. He probably needed medical attention for shock.

She flipped up the mask from the injured man's face and tipped his head back, placing one hand on his chest. His companion spoke too soon. A feeble heartbeat struggled beneath the diver's wet suit.

A warm, sticky substance oozed through her stiff fingers and she gasped. The man's wet suit sported a huge gash down the front and blood seeped from the tear. *What the heck had gone on out there?*

Amy clamped both hands against the wound to staunch the loss of blood. The man's body shuddered and jerked. His arms flew up and he grabbed her around the neck, his strong fingers creating a vise and grinding her gold chain into her neck. Choking, she clawed at his arms with her bloody hands, her nails skimming off the thick neoprene of the wet suit.

The diver behind her charged toward them and drove his knee into the man's throat. Her attacker's hands dropped from her neck and he slumped, a gush of air escaping from his lungs, a gurgle of blood spouting from the tear in his wet suit.

Amy hacked and tumbled backward, her hands hitting the sand behind her. She scrambled like a crab across the wet surface, leaving bloody indentations in her wake.

"Sorry about that." The stranger pressed his fingers against the throat of the man who'd just tried to strangle her. "Thought I had him. He's dead now."

"W-what happened to him? Why did he attack me when I was trying to save him?" She raised her gaze to the other diver, now on his knees, peeling his wet suit from the top half of his body and toeing off his fins.

He cocked his head, squinting into the fog with a steely blue gaze. "I stabbed him."

Then she noticed a knife plunged into the sand next to him. Screaming, she rolled onto her stomach and launched to her knees. A hand encircled her ankle, yanking her leg back, and she landed on her belly again. She spun around, kicking wildly with her other leg.

The man fell on top of her, covering her mouth with his hand, grinding salty grains of sand against her lips. She struggled to knee him in the crotch, but his body felt like a lead weight against her, immobilizing her.

His face inches from hers, he brought a finger to his lips. "Shh."

A chill raced up her spine. Then she heard it—the low whine of a motorboat. *Salvation.* She bucked beneath her captor and worked her jaw to open her mouth and bite his hand.

His voice growled close to her ear, his briny scent invading her nostrils. "Stop fighting me. Those are some very dangerous men out there on that boat."

His words sucked the already-diminishing air out of her lungs, and she slumped beneath his rock-hard body. She moved her lips against his palm in a silent question, the saltwater on his hand working its way into her mouth.

The maniac flashed a smile, rows of white teeth in a tanned face. They gleamed in the fog that now surrounded them like damp cotton. He winked. "Don't worry. I'm one of the good guys."

Her eyes darted to the dead diver slumped in a heap at the water's edge.

"He's one of the bad guys." He shifted his muscular frame, giving her some breathing room. "I'm going to remove my hand from your mouth and let you up, but you need to stay close to me and we need to get off this beach. Nice job on that rescue, by the way."

Amy swallowed, not even minding the sand that

scratched her throat. Two lunatics had invaded her beach and now one of them planned to kidnap her. *The perfect ending to a lousy couple of months.*

As soon as he removed his hand and his hold, she planned to scream bloody murder and run toward the sound of the boat. She could swim a long distance if she had to. Her gaze tracked over the muscled shoulders and corded arms of the man who held her, and her stomach fluttered. He could probably swim just as fast and far.

And he had a knife.

He slid his hand from her mouth, resting it on her throat. Amy dropped her gaze to the stranger's sinewy forearm and gulped. He could easily finish the job the dead guy started. As she gathered air in her lungs for a big scream, a motor whirred fast, loud and close.

In one movement, her captor rolled off her body and grabbed her arm, yanking her to her feet. At the same time, a scream ripped from her throat. A loud pop followed her cry for help and the man beside her cursed.

"Thanks a lot, beach girl. You just gave them a target in this muck."

The people on the boat confirmed his words as they fired two more shots in the general direction of Amy's head.

"Let's move." The man shoved her in front of him and she stumbled as her feet hit dry sand. At least if any more bullets came their way, they'd have to go through his large frame first. And he made a great shield.

Was he protecting her?

Keeping his hand pressed against the small of her back, he said, "This fog should give us enough cover to make it to the lifeguard truck—as long as you keep your screaming to a minimum."

Either she followed the man with the knife or turned toward the men with the guns. Since he hadn't used the knife on her—yet—and the guys on the boat insisted on shooting at vague shapes in the fog, even after she screamed, Amy put her money on the guy with the knife.

Her legs pumped in the sand. She veered toward the tower and grabbed her backpack with her sweats on top. She didn't hear any more gunshots and the occupants of the boat must've cut the motor because she couldn't hear the distinctive whine.

The thick fog almost obscured her companion. He didn't even seem to be breathing heavily, or maybe she couldn't hear him over the roaring in her ears and her own ragged breath.

He bumped her side, grabbing her upper arm. "Where's the lifeguard truck?"

"I don't have a truck on this beach. My car's parked in the lot." She tried to shake him off, but his fingers pinched harder.

"You'd better not be lying and leading me into some kind of trap. That could get us both killed." His icy blue eyes almost glowed in the fog.

"You're the one with the knife." She pried his fingers off her arm and kicked up sand behind her, hoping she got some in his face.

The beach remained eerily quiet behind them, but the dense fog could mute sounds. Amy kept up a steady pace, her feet leading her to the parking lot where her car waited. Once they got there, she'd dig her cell phone out of her backpack and call the police. The stranger couldn't object if he really was on the right side of the law.

A strip of dark asphalt appeared and Amy pointed. "It's right there."

When the soles of her feet slapped against the gritty asphalt, she swung her backpack from her shoulder and clawed for her keys in the front compartment. She clicked the remote and gasped when the man swept her in front of him, pushing her toward the car.

"Get in and drive."

Before she had a chance to figure out if she could take off without him, he scrambled into the passenger seat. He pounded the dashboard. "What are you waiting for? I said 'drive.'"

She curled her left fist around her keys and fumbled with a zipper on the backpack crushed between her lap and the bottom edge of the steering wheel. Her fingers skimmed the smooth metal of her cell phone and she pulled it out.

"I'm going to call 911 first."

His jaw hardened as he sluiced back his wet hair, beginning to curl at the ends. With a pair of broad shoulders and washboard abs that tapered to the wet suit peeled down to his slim hips, he looked like Triton or at least some sexy merman. Then he opened his mouth.

"No, you're not. We need to get out of here. Now."

Sounded like he knew his enemies well. Who was she to argue? She tossed her backpack in the backseat and started the car. "You're right. Those guys seemed determined."

A breath hitched in her throat. Maybe they were determined because they were cops or the Coast Guard, but would they start shooting into a bank of fog after she screamed without even shouting out a warning? Experience had taught her they just might. Her father had taught her to never trust the law.

Her gaze slid to the knife resting on the man's powerful thigh encased in black neoprene. She didn't have a choice right now anyway, but his reaction to her call to 911 would tell her a lot.

As she accelerated out of the beach parking lot, she scooped her cell phone from her lap where she'd dropped it and flipped it open. She'd pressed Nine before the man beside her snatched the phone from her hand.

"You can't call the cops." He cradled the phone in his palm and snapped it shut.

Amy clung to the steering wheel, her knuckles turning white. "You're going to kill me, aren't you? F-for witnessing that murder."

He tossed the phone into the backseat and let out a ragged breath. Squeezing her bare thigh with his long fingers, he said, "I'm not going to hurt you, beach girl. I'm sorry you're scared."

If he meant to soothe her with his gentle touch on her leg, it sent a ripple of fear across her skin instead. Did he plan to rape her before he murdered her?

Amy swallowed. He seemed like a fairly reasonable lunatic. Maybe she could use logic on him. "Why can't I call 911? The operator can alert the Coast Guard and go after the...the bad guys. You could be long gone by the time they picked them up, and I swear I won't tell them anything about you."

"You wouldn't be a very good lifeguard if you did that, would you?" He clicked his tongue as he rummaged through her glove compartment. He pulled out her registration and peered at it. "You can call the cops when you get home. By that time, I will be long gone and so will that dead body on the beach."

Her heart did a somersault in her chest. "When I get home?"

He flicked the paper registration with his finger. "Yeah. Drive back to your place and I'll disappear in a puff of smoke or more likely a blanket of fog."

When she'd pulled out of the beach parking lot, she'd headed in the general direction of her house since he hadn't given her any orders about where to go. Would he really let her just go home and then call the authorities after he left without hurting her?

He was right about her responsibilities as a lifeguard. She'd have to report him and give the cops as good a description as she could. She gave him a sidelong glance—over six feet tall, muscular build, a wild, tawny mane of hair that brushed his shoulders, piercing blue eyes.

She'd have to scale back on the admiration of his masculine good looks when she gave her description to the cops or they'd think she'd fallen prey to that Stockholm syndrome where victims fell for their captors.

He glanced at the registration again before shoving it back into her glove compartment. "You live close, right?"

"Yeah, we're almost there." She gripped the steering wheel with clammy hands as another thought slammed against her like a sledgehammer. He'd retrieved her registration to see her address. She did not want this dangerous man in her house, but now he knew her address. "My husband, who's six foot five and very jealous, will be home, too."

He snorted. "I'll take my chances."

"Can't I just drop you off somewhere? Why do you have to come to my house with me?"

"Just want to see you home safely." He brushed some sand off the leg of his wet suit. "Is there a work schedule posted in the tower listing the shifts for the guards?"

"N-no."

"I suppose the main station wouldn't give out the guards' names if someone called making inquiries about which guards are working which beaches?"

Her clammy grasp on the wheel got tighter. "Of course not. What are you driving at? Do you think those people in the boat will try to find out who I am?"

He lifted a shoulder, which touched the ends of his wet hair. "If they can, but it doesn't sound like they're going to be successful."

"What if they come back to that beach, that tower, looking for me? Today was my last day for the summer, but I left everything wide open back there. I'm going to have to return to close up properly."

Was he playing her to make her fear the men in the boat more than she feared him? The dying man had choked her, and the guys in the boat had shot at her. This one hadn't lifted a finger against her. In fact, he'd protected her from the other attacks.

"I don't think they'd do that." But two lines formed a deep crevice between his eyebrows. "They'd have difficulty finding the beach again, and there are plenty of lifeguard towers up and down the coast."

She chewed her bottom lip. "I don't know about that. Imperial Beach is one of the southernmost beaches in San Diego County before you hit the Mexican border."

"Request a transfer. They're not going to find you."

"They're not going to find me anyway." She rolled her tight shoulders. "I already told you. I'm done for the season since I only work summers. Today was my last shift."

He patted her leg again. "That's good to hear. And don't return. Let someone else lock up. What's your name anyway?"

"Amy." She gasped and covered her mouth. How had this man lured her into such a state of naive stupidity so quickly? Next she'd be giving him her social security number. She jerked her leg, dislodging his hand.

He had the nerve to laugh.

"Don't worry. I'm not going to use your first name against you, and I can just reach in the glove compartment to find out the rest if I want." He combed his fingers through tangled hair. "And just so we're even, I'm going to tell you my first name, too. It's Riley."

"Riley." The name rolled off her tongue. Riley didn't seem too concerned about the cops knowing his name. Did he think just because he had a friendly, non-threatening demeanor and a gorgeous body she wasn't going to report this?

Even though Amy had an innate distrust of authority, Riley had placed his confidence in the wrong woman. She'd had it in for all men since she'd discovered the guy she'd been dating for two months had a wife. *Scumbag.*

She rounded the corner of her block and pulled up to the curb in front of her rental house. She cut the engine and dropped her hands in her lap. "You can get out now. Although how you think you're going to be inconspicuous roaming around in a full-body wet suit is beyond me."

"Thanks for caring." A boyish grin claimed his face. "I have trunks on underneath—just another surfer."

"Just another surfer carrying a knife."

She shouldn't have reminded him.

His fingers curled around the handle and he said, "Let's go inside to make sure everything's okay."

Tension knotted her shoulders again as she climbed out of the car, groping for her backpack in the backseat. She wouldn't be able to breathe easily until Riley left the premises and she had 911 on the line.

It took her three tries to insert her key into the dead bolt with Riley standing behind her, the heat from his body warming her bare back. And then she didn't even need to unlock the dead bolt—she must've left it unlocked when she took off this afternoon. She shoved the key into the handle, turning the knob and pushing open the door.

Riley stepped in front of her, tucking her behind his broad frame. "Everything look okay?"

"How can I tell? I'm staring at your back." Her nose practically touched the cool, smooth skin between his shoulder blades.

Riley stalked to the center of the small living room, dwarfing it with his take-control presence. Amy shifted her gaze around the objects of the room, her pulse quickening when she spotted a book on the floor by the coffee table. Her cat, Clarence, probably knocked that over before he took off for his pre-dinner prowl.

"I'm going to have a look in the back rooms." Riley pointed to the short hallway, gripping the knife in front of him.

Amy crept toward the book and crouched to retrieve it from the floor. She glanced toward the entry that led to the kitchen and then tilted her head back to peer at Riley disappearing into the bathroom, knife still drawn.

She could make a run for the portable phone in the kitchen and slip out the back, maybe bang on her neighbor's door for help. Riley would probably take off, and she'd be safe.

Launching to her feet, she hurtled toward the kitchen. Just inside the entryway, she tripped over a soft object splayed across the floor. Yelping, she thudded against the linoleum. She scrambled to her hands and knees and spun around.

A sour knot of fear lodged in her throat as her gaze skidded across the deathly still form of her ex-boyfriend.

Chapter Two

A shriek sliced through the small house, and Riley barreled out the bathroom door, stubbing his toe on the frame. He gripped the knife at his side, ready to do battle. Careening through the empty living room, he launched toward the entryway to what had to be the kitchen. He stopped short, almost falling into the room and over a body on the floor.

Amy huddled against the cabinets, her hands pressed against her mouth, her eyes forming huge, coffee-colored saucers. A man sprawled across the faded yellow linoleum on his back, one perfectly shined loafer hanging from his toes, and his legs in pressed slacks crossed one over the other. Looked like he could be taking a nap on the kitchen floor.

Riley squatted beside the man, noting a red blotch on his right cheek, and extended two fingers toward his neck to check his pulse.

Amy screamed, "Don't touch him."

God, he must've been a friend or relative of Amy's. Boyfriend? His gaze flew to her face, drained of all color beneath her mocha skin. "Who is he?"

"Carlos...my ex-boyfriend." She mumbled through her fingers, which seemed frozen in place.

Very ex-boyfriend from the look of him. Riley stepped over the body and kneeled beside Amy. "We need to get out of here."

"What happened to him?"

"I can't tell. I don't see any blood, just a contusion on his face. Maybe someone strangled him or hit him on the back of the head." He turned back toward the body. "I can turn him..."

"No." She sobbed, curling into a tight ball. "We need to call the police."

"You don't get it, Amy. Somehow those guys in the boat tracked you down to your house. Carlos must've surprised them. They probably came at him from behind and strangled him or hit him. Carlos's presence spooked them, but that doesn't mean they won't come back."

"That's why we call the police." She scooted to her left to avoid Carlos's outstretched hand.

Riley rubbed his chin with his knuckles. He was flying so far below the radar of the police right now he couldn't afford to have them question him at a murder scene. Hell, he was flying below the radar of the CIA.

"The police can't protect you." He left the rest of that statement hanging in the air between them. Only he could protect her now, and he didn't need the encumbrance.

Surprisingly, she didn't dispute his claim.

"Who are these people? Who are you?"

"The less you know, the better." Not that he knew much himself. When the call had come from Colonel Scripps, the former leader of the undercover ops unit, Prospero, Riley had jumped into action. Jack Coburn, one of their own, had disappeared.

Riley would go through hell and back to find him.

He cupped his hand, wiggling his fingers. "Come on, beach girl. Let's go."

Amy's gaze traveled from his hand to his face. She must've seen something she liked because she sighed and pushed to her feet. He helped her over the body of her ex-boyfriend. Feeling a tremble roll through her athletic frame, Riley pulled her close and folded his arms around her.

She stiffened in his embrace and then buried her face against his bare chest as sobs wracked her body. He stroked her dark hair, clumped in wet tangles of saltwater.

Rubbing her nose, she stepped back from him and pinched her swimsuit between two fingers, yanking it forward. "Do I have time to change, or…or do you think we should get out now?"

"I don't think they'll be returning to the scene of the crime immediately." Riley crossed the room and lifted the curtains of the front window with the tip of his knife. He'd prefer a gun, but he couldn't have taken one of those with him. "They might be out there now, watching, waiting, wondering if we'll call the police."

She called from the bedroom. "I'm wondering the same thing. We can't just leave him there on the kitchen floor. H-he has a wife."

Riley swallowed. The beach girl liked married men? He cleared his throat. "We'll call the police as soon as we're out of here."

"Wait a minute." She stumbled from the bedroom in a pair of jeans, pulling a T-shirt over her head. He caught a glimpse of a lacy white bra. "Won't that look suspicious? There's a dead man in my house, and I'm not even here."

"I'll clear things up for you later. You're not safe in this house."

Her eyes narrowed as she hooked a finger along the gold chain around her neck, pulling a large locket out of her T-shirt. "*You're* not safe in this house. For whatever reason, you don't want the cops to find out about your activities. And why would you? You murdered a man on the beach and you kidnapped me."

Frustration gave an edge to his voice as he jerked his thumb toward the kitchen. "I didn't murder *him*. Don't you get it? They discovered your identity and came after you."

"They came after *you*." She hugged herself and rubbed her upper arms. "They probably figured you used me to escape. That's why they came to this house and killed Carlos. Once you get away from me, I'll be safe."

Too bad his wife hadn't figured that one out.

Pain sliced behind his eyes, and he ran a hand over his hair, clasping it in a ponytail at the nape of his neck. "You're in it, Amy, whether you want to be or not. These people don't leave loose ends."

"I'm not a loose end." She widened her stance and shoved her hands in the pockets of her jeans. "I didn't see those people. I don't know who they are. But I know who you are."

Damn. She didn't trust him. And why would she? He didn't trust himself to protect her either.

He swiped the back of his hand across his mouth. Could he leave her here? He'd take off for his safe house, and she could stay here and call the cops. She'd tell her wild story of one scuba diver killing another and people shooting at them from a boat. But there would be no body. There would be no blood. No bullets. No evidence at all.

The Velasquez Drug Cartel didn't leave evidence. Or witnesses.

Even if the cops believed Amy's fantastic story, they couldn't do much to protect her. If the Velasquez gang decided to kill her, the cops couldn't stop them.

Or maybe he'd overreacted from the get-go. From the minute she'd valiantly pulled his enemy's body from the ocean, Riley had felt protective of her. She'd only been doing her job and had landed in the middle of an international intrigue.

If he distanced himself from her now, it just might save her life. He was dangerous company.

"Okay." Riley blew out a long breath. "I'll stay with you until the cops arrive, and then I'll head out the back door."

"Really?" Her voice squeaked and her eyebrows shot up.

"Really." He tugged at the wet suit around his waist and peeled it off his body, standing on one foot at a time to free his legs from the constricting neoprene. "What are you going to tell the police?"

Her gaze raked his body as her chest rose and fell. "The truth."

"The guys on the boat will have removed the body of their comrade and my scuba gear from the beach by now." He nudged the wet suit lying in a twisted heap on the carpet. "I can leave this here if you think it will bolster your story."

"Why would I need to bolster my story?" She dragged her gaze from his wet trunks, meeting his eyes, a pleasing shade of pink washing over her cheeks.

The beach girl had been checking him out. And he liked it.

Riley's fingers plowed through his long hair. "You plan to report a murder on the beach with no body. Your ex-boyfriend is dead on your kitchen floor with no signs of a struggle or break-in. Why is he your ex? Bad breakup?"

"No. Yes." She folded her arms across her stomach. "He lied to me about being married."

Riley whistled through his teeth. "Do you have a history of violence?"

"Not yet." Amy clenched her fists and took a step toward him.

"I'm just sayin'." A strange sense of relief flooded his veins. He knew a valiant woman like Amy wouldn't knowingly get mixed up with a married man.

"Do you think they'll suspect me of murdering Carlos? I'm pretty strong, but not strong enough to strangle a man. I broke it off as soon as I discovered his marital status. Why would I kill him and then call the cops? It would look much worse if I ran out now, wouldn't it?"

She covered her face with her hands, and guilt stabbed his belly. He didn't want her to feel worse. He wanted to smooth everything over and make sure she kept safe after he left.

He tripped over the wet suit as he rushed to her side and curled an arm around her shoulders. She leaned into him. Her T-shirt felt soft against his bare chest, brushing a tingle of desire along his skin.

Her salty hair tickled his lips as he spoke. "Just tell the truth. You'll be fine. There's no evidence that you killed Carlos even if the police find your story unbelievable."

"C-can't you stay and talk to the cops with me?" She clutched his arm, her nails digging into his skin.

"I wish I could help you out, beach girl, but I can't afford the time if they decide to arrest me." He couldn't afford the exposure either. Having his picture splashed all over the newspapers in connection with two murders would torpedo any chance he'd have to follow his lead on the Velasquez Cartel and any of its customers.

And right now the Velasquez lead was the only thread they had in connection with Jack Coburn's disappearance.

Amy took a shaky breath and stepped back. "You're not going to tell me anything else, are you?"

"No."

"Then you'd better get ready to leave so I can call 911. I can't bear to be here with Carlos like that." Her bottom lip quivered, and her dark eyes brimmed with unshed tears.

Riley cupped her face with one hand, smoothing the pad of his thumb across her cheekbone. "I'm sorry about Carlos. What do you think he was doing here?"

At his touch, she'd closed her eyes, but now her eyelids flew open, droplets of tears trembling on the edges of her long lashes. "Huh?"

"Carlos. Why was he in your house and how did he get in? Did you give him a key?"

"I gave him a key once to feed my cat when I was gone for the weekend. But he gave it back to me."

"He made a copy."

Her eyes widened. "He wouldn't do that."

"Really? The man entered your home while you were

at work. I thought you broke up with him a few months ago?"

"I did." She wiped her palms on the thighs of her jeans.

"Did he contact you after the breakup?"

"A few times but..." Her arms flailed at her sides.

"Face it, Amy. The guy never got over you. He probably came here hoping he could change your mind. Didn't work out too well for him."

She dug her fists in her hips. "The back door is in the kitchen. You can leave before the cops get here."

"If he made a copy of your key, it's probably still in his pocket. Do you want me to take it?"

"So you can have a key to my place? No, thanks. Why would I want you to take the key? I don't want to disturb a crime scene."

"Too late for that. You changed clothing and you didn't notify the police as soon as you discovered the body." He shrugged. "I'm just thinking it might look better for you if the dead ex-boyfriend didn't still have a key to your house."

"Okay. You know what?" She grabbed his arm and dragged him toward the kitchen. "There's the back door. Use it."

Instead he crouched next to the body and slid his hand into the front pocket of the man's expensive slacks. His nostrils flared at the sweet scent emanating from his clothing. Carlos liked his cologne strong.

Nothing in that pocket except a few bills. Riley reached for the other pocket, but he didn't have to go digging. Carlos's keychain was on the floor by the pocket. Riley's fingers closed around the silver ring and he dangled it from his index finger.

"Is this your key?" A removable ring was hanging from the main keychain, and he shook it in front of Amy's face.

"It could be. What difference does it make? Now you've corrupted the crime scene even more. Put it back and get out, and maybe you should leave some more of your fingerprints around here so the cops can identify you…Riley…if that's even your name."

"I didn't touch anything in here." He twirled the keychain around his finger. "Except you."

Amy's eyes glittered, shooting gold sparks, but a soft rose color swept across her cheeks. Stepping behind him to avoid the body on the floor, she grabbed the knob to the back door. She turned quickly, her hair whipping across his chest. "What will you do for clothes?"

Still clutching the keychain, Riley adjusted the waistband of his board shorts while her gaze tracked his movements feeling like a whisper of fingertips. "We're a mile from the beach—nothing unusual about someone walking around in swim trunks. If you give me a couple of bucks for the bus, that would make my life a lot easier."

"Gladly." She slipped past him and snagged her backpack from the coffee table where she'd dropped it. She groped inside a side compartment and gasped. "My wallet."

"It's gone?"

"It must've fallen out in the sand when I grabbed my pack from the tower."

"That explains how the bad guys found you."

"But how'd they get here so fast?" She hugged the backpack to her chest.

"The men who killed Carlos aren't the same men who

shot at us on the beach. This is an organization, not a few petty crooks."

She swayed and he caught her. "Are you sure you don't want to get out of here with me?" Riley asked.

"No. I want to call the police. Th-they'll keep me safe."

Even she didn't sound like she believed that. If Amy expected the San Diego Sheriff's Department to put a twenty-four-hour guard on her, she didn't understand how police departments operated. That would happen only if they arrested her for the murder of her ex.

Riley could protect her. He knew the danger she faced, but he couldn't drag her out of her house if she didn't want to go. And she clearly didn't want to go.

He brushed her knotted hair from her face. "Okay, beach girl. You call the cops and stay safe."

"Hold on." She spun around and rummaged through a purse on the desk by the front window. She withdrew her hand, clutching several bills between her fingers. "Take this. And you stay safe, too."

His hand covered hers and he drew her close. She smelled like the sea, tangy and fresh. He had bent his head to brush her lips with his when a movement outside the window caught his attention.

With a grunt, Riley threw both of his arms around Amy. As they tumbled to the floor, she opened her mouth to scream. He clapped his hand across her lips for the second time that day.

Chapter Three

He'd fooled her. He planned to kill her and had just been stringing her along for his sadistic pleasure.

She was batting a thousand—a married man and now a killer.

Riley brushed her ear with a whisper. "They're outside."

His words sent a river of chills down her spine, and she reflexively dug her nails into his back.

"Stay low." Riley heaved to a crouching position and tugged at the waistband of her jeans. "Let's go out the back."

Amy slid across the floor on her belly, twisting her head toward the front window. Adrenaline charged through her body when she saw the outline of a gun.

She wriggled faster, like a snake shedding its skin. When she reached the kitchen, she gagged at the sight of Carlos on the floor.

Riley rose to his haunches. "Get the back door."

Turning the knob, she eased open the door, scooping in deep breaths of fresh air. Riley bumped her outside and told her to close the door behind them. He really didn't want to leave any fingerprints in her house.

She grabbed his hand, pulling him toward the small backyard. "This way."

They dashed across the lawn, the wet grass sticking to her feet in their flimsy flip-flops. Riley cinched her around the waist and hoisted her up the fence. She clambered over and fell into her neighbor's yard. Riley swooped over the fence after her.

"Let's keep running and hope we don't meet a dog."

She yanked on the hem of his board shorts. "Do you still have those keys you took out of Carlos's pocket?"

He patted his own pocket. "Yep."

"He used to park his car on the side street. We can get to it from here without going to the front of the house."

"You're brilliant, beach girl." He grabbed her head with both hands and kissed her forehead.

Not exactly the kiss she'd anticipated in the house, but it would do—for now.

They crouched at the side of the house behind hers, then charged through the gate, stumbling into her neighbor's front yard.

"This street." She pointed to the left and they hit the sidewalk running. Two kids playing basketball with a garage hoop looked up and snickered as they jogged by.

They reached the corner and Riley held her back. "Hang on."

He peered both ways down the street. "It's clear. Which car is his?"

She pointed to Carlos's black BMW parked at the curb. When they'd dated, she'd always wondered why he'd preferred to park his car on the street around the corner from her house. He'd told her there was less traffic on this street, and he'd wanted to protect his car. He'd really wanted to protect himself.

Guess that hadn't worked out for him today.

"On the count of three, sprint for the car." Riley held up the keys. "I won't hit the remote until we get there... just in case they're closer than we think."

Amy kicked off her flip-flops and scooped them up from the sidewalk with one hand. Holding her breath, she waited for Riley's signal. At three, she shot off as if she was heading into the ocean for a rescue.

The car alarm beeped once, and she grabbed the handle and dropped onto the leather seat. Before she closed the door, the car lurched forward and Riley careened around the corner. Panting, Amy twisted in her seat. No headlights followed them.

She snapped on her seat belt and leaned against the headrest, closing her eyes. "Where to?"

"I can drop you off at the police station or at least down the block from the police station. Then you can report everything, and they'll come back to the house with you. Those men won't try anything with the cops there."

She stuffed her feet into her flip-flops. "What about when the cops leave?"

"Can you stay with someone for a few days until this blows over? Chances are once Carlos's killers realize you don't know anything, and you keep your distance from me, they'll leave you alone."

"Chances are?" She gripped the edge of the seat, her damp hands slipping off the leather.

"Those boys have bigger fish to fry to risk going after a witness who may or may not even be a witness."

"All right then. Take me to the police station." She knotted her fingers in her lap. "What should I tell them… about you, I mean?"

His boyish grin danced across his face. "Tell them the truth. I have a feeling nothing-but will do for you."

"I'll tell them you saved my life…twice."

He cocked his head. "Are you always so loyal?"

"I don't know about that. If you're telling me the truth, you don't need to be locked up in a jail cell while the cops try to figure out your involvement and degree of culpability. Sometimes the cops aren't too particular."

He squeezed her clenched hands with a firm grasp. "Don't worry about me, beach girl. The cops aren't going to find me."

She glanced at his large hand, brown from the sun, his calluses rough against her skin. "What are you, Riley?"

"I told you before, the less you know, the better. This way you don't have to lie to the cops."

She snorted. "I don't mind lying to the cops if there's a good reason. Where will you go after you drop me off? You're not finished with those men, are you?"

His mouth formed a thin line as he fumbled with Carlos's built-in GPS. Amy sighed. She'd never know anything more about him than his name—and how his body felt against hers, shielding her, protecting her.

"There's a police station pretty close. I'll drop you off down the block, watch you go inside, and then I'll be out of your life."

She swallowed. "What are you going to do with Carlos's car?"

"I'll leave it someplace where it can be recovered and

returned to his…wife." He raised one eyebrow. "How'd that happen anyway?"

Hunching her shoulders, Amy clasped her hands between her knees. "I met him at the beach while I was working. We went out a few times from there. He came to my place a few times…"

She clenched her jaw. She didn't want to waste her last few minutes with Riley talking about her train wreck of a love life. "You know, I never thanked you for saving me on the beach. And if you hadn't come back with me to my house, that man outside with the gun could've killed me."

"It's the least I could do." He brushed his fingers along her arm. "I put you in danger by landing on your beach."

Every time Riley touched her, she felt a current of electricity run through her body. She'd better turn that off. This mysterious man would be disappearing from her life in a matter of minutes.

She rubbed her eyes. "Didn't look like you had much choice."

Drawing his brows together, he scratched his chin. "Yeah. I don't know why they decided to anchor off the coast at that particular spot. But I plan to find out."

Amy's heart galloped in her chest. Riley was a man who lived dangerously—and seemed to enjoy it. Just her type. She'd tried and tried to gravitate toward stable men with stable jobs, but it never seemed to work out. Carlos had his own import/export business, but he hadn't turned out to be dependable either. Maybe her excitement radar had somehow picked up on that, too.

The car slowed and Riley pulled into the parking lot

of a strip mall. "There's the police station. I'll watch from here until you're safely inside."

Amy rubbed her tingling nose. Once she got rid of Riley she'd be safe. Wouldn't she? She grabbed the door handle.

His hand dropped to her shoulder, and she twisted around. He slid his fingers up to her throat, his eyes now a dark blue, clouding over like a stormy sea. Her pulse ticked wildly beneath his touch.

"Be careful, beach girl." Then he cupped the back of her head and drew her close, sealing his lips over hers.

The quick kiss didn't feel like goodbye. It felt like a protective stamp that she'd carry with her forever.

She managed an inarticulate goodbye as she scrambled out of the car. Walking toward the police station, she didn't dare turn around, even though she could feel Riley's gaze searing her back.

God, she hoped the police could help her, even though she didn't trust them. She hoped for once they could reassure her and make her feel safe.

As safe as she'd felt with Riley.

RILEY EXHALED HIS PENT-UP breath as Amy swung open the glass door of the San Diego Sheriff's Station and disappeared inside.

Velasquez's people murdered Carlos because they expected Riley to show up there with Amy. Why didn't they just wait there? Why did they leave then return? Carlos must've upset their plans even though it didn't look like the guy put up much of a fight.

He rolled his shoulders and put the car in gear. Once Amy returned with the sheriff's deputies, Velasquez's men would realize Riley had taken flight. Then they'd leave Amy alone.

They'd better leave Amy alone.

He swung the sleek car back onto Imperial Beach Boulevard and accelerated toward the highway. He had to get back to that beach to find out why it had been such a strategic location for the Velasquez Cartel. The boat hadn't moored off that coast and sent a diver in by accident.

If the guy hadn't spotted him and attacked him underwater, Riley could have surprised a meeting or interrupted a drop. Maybe their fight had scared off the contact on the beach.

He smacked the leather steering wheel with the heels of his hands. He'd have to wait until morning anyway. The cops would most likely follow Amy back to the scene of the crime and light up that beach like a Christmas tree.

Until they realized there was no evidence of a crime. No evidence. No crime.

They'd find plenty of evidence at Amy's house though. Really sucked for Carlos. Should be a warning to married men everywhere not to cheat.

Although, after spending a few hours with Amy, he could understand the temptation Carlos had faced.

A buzzing noise filled the car, and Riley almost swerved into the next lane. Tilting his head, he determined the sound was coming from the backseat. Cell phone?

He took the next exit and swung into an empty parking lot next to some train tracks. He unsnapped his seat belt, twisting in his seat. A small light glowed from the pocket of a jacket on the backseat. Riley reached over, slid his hand in the pocket and pulled out the cell phone, flashing Missed Call.

The guy's wife? He flipped open the phone and checked the display, which read Restricted. The caller hadn't bothered to leave a voice mail or text message either.

Riley glanced at the clock on the dashboard. He had to check in with the colonel. Might as well use Carlos's phone before dumping it. He wouldn't need it, and his wife probably wouldn't care to see all those calls to Amy.

The colonel picked up on the first ring.

"Colonel, it's Riley."

"Did you get anything from the lead on that boat?"

"A couple of dead bodies. The boat dropped anchor off the coast near Imperial Beach and sent in a diver. Let's just say we mixed it up a little before we reached the shore. He could've been meeting someone or scouting the location. I didn't stick around to find out because his buddies started shooting at us."

"Us?"

"There was a lifeguard on the beach."

The colonel swore. "Is he okay?"

"*She's* okay." And then Riley reported what had occurred, taking full responsibility for the screwup.

The colonel swore again. "You're going to have to go back to that beach and figure out why it's important to the Velasquez crew."

"Any more news about Jack?" Riley held his breath.

"The CIA is calling him a traitor. They're convinced he's working for the other side."

Riley choked on his bitter rage. "That's not possible. You know it and I know it."

"I know Jack Coburn's name came up in chatter between the Velasquez Drug Cartel and an arms dealer in Colorado. Find out the link between those two, Riley, and we might be on the first step to finding Jack and proving his innocence."

"I'm on it. I owe Jack."

"We all do. I have another name to give you—Castillo. My CIA contact slipped it to me. He's connected to the Velasquez boys. And one more thing, I'm giving you a new number for me."

As the colonel rattled off the number, Riley lunged for the glove compartment. He groped in the dark recess, and his fingers tripped across a pen and a scrap of paper as other papers floated to the floor of the car. He jotted down the colonel's new number and ended the call.

Glancing at the cell phone in his hand, he realized he couldn't leave the phone in Carlos's car for the police to find. Not that the colonel had an even remotely traceable phone number, but just like the fingerprints in Amy's house, he wanted to err on the side of caution. That included the fingerprints in this car. He'd wipe it clean before abandoning it.

Then he'd get back to his safe house, claim his own car and skulk outside Amy's house after the cops left just to make sure she got off to her friends' house okay.

He pressed his knuckle against the switch for the dome light and bent forward to retrieve the papers from the car mat. A few receipts. A scribbled address. Registration.

Pinching the corner of the registration between two

fingers, Riley raised it to the light. He read the name aloud. "Carlos Castillo."

Castillo.

The name slammed against his brain, and bright spots danced in front of his eyes. Amy's ex hadn't been the victim of bad luck. Carlos had chosen Amy for a reason. The Velasquez cartel had chosen that beach for a reason. Someone killed Carlos Castillo for a reason.

And now they might have a reason to kill Amy.

AMY GULPED IN A LUNGFUL of the damp evening air as she squared off with the San Diego Sheriff's deputy. She pointed a shaky finger toward her house. "His body was on my kitchen floor. He was dead."

"Ms. Prescott, can you explain to us how, not one, but two dead bodies can disappear in one night?" Deputy Sampson crossed his arms over his chest.

He and another sheriff's deputy had accompanied her to the beach, and just as Riley had predicted, someone had collected the body of the diver and Riley's diving gear. In the meantime, the sheriff's department had sent another car to Amy's house to check on the dead body of Carlos Castillo. Amy hadn't expected that one to disappear, too.

Why? Why would this drug cartel remove Carlos's body?

She closed her eyes. Maybe she had dreamed the entire episode. She licked her lips, still salty from Riley's kiss, and knew she'd been wide awake.

"Call Carlos's wife. I'm sure she'll verify that he's missing."

Deputy Sampson slipped a phone out of his pocket. "What's the number?"

"I—I don't know his home number, just his cell."

"What's that then?"

"I don't know that either. I can't remember it, and I deleted it from my contacts."

The deputy rolled his eyes, and Amy clenched her jaw to keep from screaming. She ground out between clenched teeth, "Why would I lie about a couple of dead bodies and a mysterious spy?"

"Look, Ms. Prescott. I'm not saying you're lying, but there's not much we can do right now with no bodies to back up your story and your, uh, spy nowhere to be found." He jerked his thumb over his shoulder. "Maybe Mr. Castillo wasn't dead, and he got up and walked away."

"He was dead." She clenched her hands in front of her, recalling that she wouldn't let Riley touch Carlos's body. "H-he looked dead."

"Maybe you did stumble on some kind of drug deal. God knows, this close to the Mexican border we've seen plenty of crap going down. We'll send someone out to the beach again tomorrow. The body just might wash up on shore. And obviously if we get a call from Mrs. Castillo reporting a missing husband, we'll be back."

Another deputy jogged down her front steps. "If someone did snatch the body, whoever it was did a great cleanup job."

"And what about the wet suit?" Amy shoved her hands in the back pockets of her jeans. Not that she wanted to put the cops on Riley's trail, but a little bit of evidence might show she hadn't been delusional.

"Did you find the wet suit on the living room floor?" Deputy Sampson jerked his chin toward the other deputy.

"No. There's some sand around, but isn't she a life-guard who just got off work?"

Amy stamped her foot, feeling about two years old. "I'm not making this up. A man saved my life on the beach and came home with me. He's the one who dropped me off at the station."

"Did you have a bad breakup with this ex-boyfriend of yours, Ms. Prescott? You found out he was married, you went a little crazy?" He held up his hands. "Hey, I don't blame you. Maybe you changed your mind and you wanted him back. He'd rush to your rescue or something, leave his wife."

Amy's jaw dropped. "That is so not me, Deputy Sampson."

He lifted his shoulders as the other two deputies ambled toward their squad cars parked at the curb, their red lights still casting a glow over the few neighbors who'd remained outside during the excitement.

Amy rubbed her arms. This was it. They were leaving. They didn't believe her, or they strongly doubted her. Thought she was some love-obsessed loon.

"I'll tell you what." Deputy Sampson shoved his useless little notebook in his pocket. "Like I said, we'll send someone to check out the beach tomorrow. In the meantime, I'll look into the whereabouts of Carlos Castillo. If he's missing, we'll be back."

"I probably won't be here." She squared her shoulders. "I'm not going to stick around to see if they bring the body back. You don't plan to stick around—do you?"

"I'm sorry, Ms. Prescott. We're not in the bodyguard business, but I'll make sure a patrol car takes a couple of turns around your neighborhood tonight."

Yeah, that makes me feel warm and fuzzy. Amy

gripped her upper arms. It didn't matter. These sheriff's deputies with their rolling eyes and tight-lipped suspicions didn't make her feel safe anyway. Only one man could make her feel safe right now—Riley, her phantom spy.

She pointed to Deputy Sampson's notebook, now tucked away in his pocket. "You have my cell phone number. I'll probably be spending a few days with some friends."

"Good idea."

With their so-called investigation wrapped up, the cops scrambled for their squad cars and started their engines. Amy turned her back on her neighbors' curious stares and slammed the front door of her rental house. She couldn't bring herself to go into the kitchen to make a cup of tea.

How could there be no evidence of a dead body? *Professionals.* Riley had warned her about these drug dealers. But Carlos's wife would miss him and contact the police. Then they'd come running back here with the smirks wiped off their officious faces.

Right now she planned to get out of there. Riley had tried to reassure her that the murderous thugs were after him, not her, but those same murderous thugs had slipped into her house while she was gone and stolen the dead body of her ex-boyfriend. Not a good sign.

She'd spend a few days with Sarah and Cliff. She didn't figure she'd have much luck rounding up her cat, Clarence, tonight. Maybe she'd leave a note for the girl down the street to put out food for him in her absence.

Amy crept down the hallway toward her bedroom, flipping on all the lights. She perched at the end of her bed and reached for the phone. She called Sarah and Cliff and got the babysitter.

"Could you ask them to call me as soon as they get home? It doesn't matter how late."

Amy dragged a suitcase from her hall closet and heaved it on top of her bed. She scooped up an armful of shorts and jeans and shoved them into the bag. She threw open her closet door and swept T-shirts and sweaters from their hangers.

After cramming everything in the suitcase, including her damp lifeguard swimsuit, she headed for the bathroom. She dumped some toiletries into a small bag and spun around.

Right into the solid form of a naked man.

A scream gathered in Amy's lungs, but before she could let loose, she realized the naked man was only half-naked—and he was no stranger.

"Riley! What are you doing here? The cops just left, and they didn't believe more than half of my story, especially since Carlos's body is gone."

He gripped her shoulders, his fingers pinching her flesh. "You need to get out, Amy."

She swung the toiletry bag from her arm. "That's what I'm doing."

"I mean you need to leave now, with me."

"W-what are you talking about?"

"Your ex-boyfriend, Carlos Castillo, wasn't who he said he was."

"I know that. He was married."

"It's worse than that, Amy. He was involved with the Velasquez Drug Cartel. And now so are you."

Chapter Four

A jolt speared Amy's chest and she sucked in a sharp breath. "I don't believe you. Why are you saying this?"

"My...associate gave me his name. Carlos Castillo, right?" Riley tightened his grip on her shoulders and gave her a shake.

Squeezing her eyes shut, she nodded. She hadn't told him Carlos's last name. As her heartbeat raced, her mind slowed to a sluggish crawl. Her tongue felt thick and numb in her mouth. She didn't want to move. She didn't want to face any of it. Hadn't she endured enough drama in her life already from her childhood?

"I'm sorry." Riley released his grip and rubbed her upper arms. "I'm worried about you. What was Carlos doing here? Why did he single you out?"

"I don't know." Amy dragged her hands through her tangled hair and blew out a breath, expelling all her self-pity with it.

She straightened her spine. "It must have something to do with the beach. That's where we met. He must've sought me out there for a reason."

"Hold that thought." Riley grabbed the toiletry bag from her hand and charged past her into the bedroom. He dropped the bag into the open suitcase and glanced over his shoulder. "You have everything you need? I'm getting you out of here."

It looked like she had everything she needed standing right beside the bed. Riley knew how to take control of a situation and obviously relished the challenge. "I was waiting for a call from my friends before heading over to their place."

"How about you head over to my place for now? With what you know and what I know, maybe we can figure out your level of involvement in this mess." He zipped up her suitcase and hauled it off the bed.

She tilted her head. "You're going to tell me what you know?"

Shrugging, he yanked up the handle on her bag and wheeled it out the door as she stepped aside. "You're in it up to your pretty chin, so you deserve to know what's going on. And I'm relieved to find out I'm not responsible for your involvement or Carlos's death."

He thought she had a pretty chin? She rubbed it and then clenched her teeth. "I'm glad the fact that Carlos targeted me for some kind of criminal enterprise is making you feel warm and fuzzy inside."

Riley grinned, and then she felt warm and sticky inside. If she had to take off into the wild unknown with drug dealers pursuing her, at least she had a hot guy along for the ride.

"You know what I mean." He pointed to the front door. "I still have Carlos's car. Let's use that instead of yours."

She held up her index finger. "Hang on. I need to leave a note for the neighbor girl to feed my cat."

As she scribbled the note, Riley flung open the front

door and peered into the darkness. "It's all clear. Where does the girl live?"

"Two doors down." She waved the piece of paper stuck to her finger with tape.

She jogged down the sidewalk and slapped the note on the outside of the mailbox. Poor Clarence must've high tailed it out of there when Carlos came calling. Her cat never liked Carlos. She should've paid more attention to his feline instincts.

She joined Riley at the rear of the BMW. He popped the trunk and heaved the suitcase inside. "When we get to my house, we'll search the car. I haven't had time yet."

"Looks like you haven't had time for anything." Amy allowed her gaze to wander down his body to his swim trunks, now dry and hanging loosely from his slim hips. The muscles of his flat belly clenched as he slammed down the trunk.

He tugged at a stiff lock of her hair. "You, either. When we get to my place, we can take a shower."

Her cheeks warmed, and Riley lifted one brow. "One at a time."

How'd he see her blush in the dark? Unless the same naughty thought had popped into his head.

As she slid onto the passenger seat, Amy drew her eyebrows together. She must be overcoming her trust issues—by leaps and bounds—since she'd accepted Riley's story so readily. Something about the man instilled confidence—and a whole lot more.

Of course, she'd been willing to trust Carlos, too, and look where that had landed her. Or had she? She'd never let Carlos completely into her life. She'd never slept with him. He had accused her so many times of holding back. That's why she was surprised when she'd discovered his marital status. Usually men cheated on their wives so they could sleep around, not hold hands and walk on the beach.

Unless those men were sinister drug dealers with ulterior motives. Carlos probably didn't even have a wife.

Riley hit the highway and accelerated. "So the cops didn't believe you?"

"It's like you said." She slumped in the leather seat. "They didn't find anything at the beach, and then when we got to my place, someone had removed Carlos's body."

"Did they question you about me?" He slid a sidelong glance at her.

She snorted. "They thought I'd watched too many James Bond movies."

He smiled, but she heard him release a long breath. "I wonder why they took Carlos, and how. You'd think your neighbors would've noticed people dragging a dead body from your house."

"Lots of older folks in that neighborhood, not much activity at night. So how'd you find out about Carlos's connection to the drug dealers?"

"I saw his registration minutes after my contact gave me his name. It makes sense, but it doesn't explain what he was doing at your house at the time of the drop, or why his associates killed him. What can you tell me about Carlos?"

Amy curled a leg beneath her and gazed out the window. "I met him before summer started. He was charming and interesting and he kept coming back to my beach. We started dating and then I discovered he had a wife."

"How'd that happen?"

It sounded so petty now, but any information she could give Riley might help. Amy cleared her throat. "I—I didn't trust Carlos. Some of his actions seemed suspicious—the parking around the corner, the excuses for never meeting at his place, the endless cell phone calls. So one day I answered his cell phone."

Riley reached over and tucked a stray lock of hair behind her ear. "Don't look so sheepish. You had good reason to suspect him and you followed your instincts. Who'd you find on the other end, the wife?"

"Yep." She clasped her hands between her knees. "Of course, now I'm not so sure. For a wife, she didn't seem very upset that another woman had just answered her husband's cell phone."

"Did you confront Carlos?"

"I did and he admitted it. I immediately ended the relationship."

Riley drummed his thumbs on the steering wheel and narrowed his eyes. "She could've been the real deal. Drug dealers get married, too."

"I guess." She lifted a shoulder. "So why do you think he hooked up with me in the first place?"

"He wanted access to that beach." His lips quirked in a quick grin. "Not that you aren't without your charms."

Amy rolled her eyes. "Don't worry. No offense taken."

"He probably wanted to find out about lifeguard schedules and procedures and pass the information on to the guys in the boat."

"He did ask a lot of questions, which seemed natural at the time. But what was he doing back at my place tonight, why'd his associates kill him and why'd they come back for me…or you?"

"And now you're asking a lot of questions, none of which I can answer."

"How about I start asking some you can answer?" Amy shifted in her seat and studied Riley's profile. This man with his ready grin and sarcastic quips could turn lethal in a matter of seconds. His dark blue eyes could shine with humor and cloud over with secrets just as fast. She wanted to dig deeper to solve the enigma of Riley…. Riley. She didn't even know his last name.

"I'll answer anything you like once I've had a shower and something to eat." He jerked his thumb toward the window. "We're here."

Riley wheeled the car into the parking lot of a non-descript apartment complex. Amy didn't know what she expected for a safe house, but a sprawling apartment building in the middle of San Diego didn't exactly fit the bill for a secret agent.

Riley pulled into a numbered parking slot. "Good thing I stole Carlos's car since I left mine down by the harbor."

"It won't be such a good thing if Carlos's wife reported the car stolen."

Riley grabbed the door handle and raised his brows. "If Carlos had a wife."

Amy scrambled from the car while Riley unlocked the trunk. She joined him at the rear of the car as he yanked her suitcase from the back and set it on its wheels. Then he ducked back inside the trunk, sweeping his hands across its surface.

"Doesn't look like Carlos kept anything in here, but he left his jacket in the backseat along with his cell phone. We can take a closer look at the phone once we're inside." He slammed the trunk closed and locked up again.

Amy liked the sound of that. Riley really did plan to include her. Must be because the drug cartel had put her directly in their line of fire.

Every crisis had a silver lining.

She followed Riley to the elevator as he dragged her bag behind him. He had a small place tucked away in the corner on the third floor of the building.

He threw open the door for her, and she stepped into the apartment that had the look and feel of a standard motel. Serviceable furniture populated the living room and small dining area. The blank walls stared back at her.

"Homey place." She tossed her purse onto one of two matching gray chairs.

"The agency isn't known for its decorating skills."

"So you're working for the CIA?" Amy swallowed against her dry throat. Not great news, but she'd rather be on the run with a CIA agent than an FBI agent. Any day.

"Not exactly." He dumped Carlos's keychain in a basket on the kitchen counter. "They're financing this operation, but they don't know it."

"That's kind of them. So what are you, an undercover agent?" She liked the sound of that even better. Maybe she had watched too many Bond movies.

"Me?" That sexy grin spread across his face again, made sexier by the stubble on his chin. "I run a dive boat in Mexico. Cabo San Lucas, to be exact."

Tilting her head, Amy put her hands on her hips. "You're just messing with me now."

"God's honest truth." He held up his fingers, Boy

Scout—style, but Amy doubted his Boy Scout credentials, especially when that dangerous glint lit up his blue eyes.

Riley yanked up the handle of her suitcase and dragged it toward the back of the apartment. "Take a shower, and I'll whip up something to eat. It's almost midnight. You must be as hungry as I am."

Amy's stomach growled to punctuate his comment. Maybe she could blame hunger for making her weak in the knees instead of Riley's devil-may-care grin. "I'm starving, but then we talk."

"Deal."

He disappeared through a door, and Amy followed him into a small bedroom. The neatly made bed dominated the room and for one crazy moment, she wanted to pull those covers over her head and sleep for about a week.

Riley wheeled her bag into a corner and then grabbed a T-shirt from a hanger in the closet. He pointed to another door across the hall. "The bathroom's in there and the towels are in the cupboard. Leave some hot water for me."

He clicked the door behind him and Amy fell across the bed. *Safety.*

RILEY DROPPED FOUR pieces of bacon onto the paper towel and blotted the grease from the strips as his belly rumbled. Inhaling the salty aroma of the bacon, he broke off an edge and popped it into his watering mouth.

He whistled while he whisked the eggs, halting in midrambling tune when he heard the shower finally stop. Amy must've thought he was kidding about that hot water.

But then she needed a warm shower more than he did. She'd held up well under the stress of the situation—no crying, screaming or gnashing of teeth—but the pallor beneath her sun-kissed skin and her wide dark eyes hinted at her fear. Or anger. The woman definitely had an edge—and he liked it.

Several minutes later, as he crumbled the bacon on top of the bubbling eggs, the bedroom door swung open and Amy tiptoed into the living room.

"Everything still okay?"

Riley concentrated on flipping the omelet. "Did you think the Velasquez Drug Cartel was in here cooking eggs and bacon?"

"You never know." She huffed out a breath and sauntered to the kitchen counter. "They could've surprised you mid-egg and then enjoyed the fruits of your labor over your dead body."

He laughed and slid the omelet onto the waiting plate. "You have a twisted way of thinking, Amy Prescott."

"How'd you know my last name?" She clutched the edge of the counter, her knuckles turning white.

Guess that warm shower didn't do much to relax her. His gaze raked her from head to toe, taking in the warm mahogany hair falling over one shoulder and those long legs encased in the same faded denim she'd worn earlier.

"Relax, beach girl. It didn't take a trained observer to see the tag on your backpack. I thought you trusted me now. I made omelets."

"Omelets are the new olive branch or something?" She sniffed the air. "They smell good. I guess I'll have to suspend suspicion to eat."

"That's a start. And to make things even, my name's

Riley Hammond." He snagged two forks from a drawer and slid a plate toward her. "I'm going to hit the shower. I've been wearing these board shorts longer than a man should wear anything."

Except a long lean woman like Amy.

Riley compressed his lips as if he'd spoken his thought aloud. Amy, gazing longingly at the plate, hadn't noticed his shift from protector to wolf.

"Do you want me to wait until you're out of the shower?" She pointed the tines of the fork at the omelet.

"Nah. This ain't the Ritz. Dig in."

He grabbed a clean towel from the closet and crossed the hall to the bathroom.

As he pulled the door behind him, Amy called out, "Don't close it."

He twisted around, raising his brows.

Two spots of color brightened her cheeks. "I—I'd just feel better with the door open. I promise I won't peek."

Too bad.

"You'd better not." He shook his finger at her. "Because I'm really modest."

Amy cackled and stabbed her omelet.

Riley cranked on the shower and bent forward as he flattened his palms against the tile. The warm water cascaded down his back, and he rolled his shoulders. As he lathered his hair and body, thoughts of Amy poked and prodded him.

He didn't need a companion to do his job, especially one as distracting as Amy. Even though Carlos had dragged her into this situation, Riley wanted to keep her well away from it. And well away from him.

If his wife, April, had steered clear of him, she'd be alive. But Amy was made of stronger stuff than April. Riley lifted his face to the spray of suddenly cold water to punish himself for his disloyal thoughts about April.

She was dead and had taken their unborn baby with her. Their deaths had compelled him to banish all the resentment he'd felt toward her for tricking him into a marriage he didn't want. And he had to keep that resentment at bay or fall into a black hole of never-ending guilt.

"Your cell phone is buzzing."

Riley shut off the water and cracked open the shower door. Amy's hand, clutching his phone, wiggled in the bathroom doorway.

"Can you bring it over before I miss the call?" He sluiced back his hair.

Holding the vibrating phone in front of her, she stumbled into the bathroom with eyes squeezed shut. She tripped over the toilet, banging her knee on the lid.

"Don't let your embarrassment be the death of you." He crossed one arm in front of his body and held out his other hand for the phone.

Amy peeled her eyes open and pinned her gaze to his face as she handed him the phone. Once he had it in hand, she whipped around and scurried out of the bathroom.

Swallowing hard, he slid the phone open with his wet hand. "Hello?"

"Hope I didn't wake you." The colonel's gruff voice doused any desire Riley had felt over Amy's intrusion.

"I'm in the shower. It's been a long day."

"Hate to make it longer, but I thought you were going to check out that beach."

"I'll be on it tomorrow, Colonel. You know I'm accustomed to Jack's hands-off leadership." Riley pulled a towel from the rack and slung it over his shoulder, his eyes darting to the door Amy had left wide open.

"Yeah, I know. The ends justify the means and all that. Maybe that's how Jack got into trouble. Did you go back to the beach?"

Riley's jaw clenched at the colonel's criticism of Jack. Colonel Scripps hadn't been on the front line with them. Although the colonel had served his time, he filled the role of paper pusher now. He didn't understand that Jack's leadership fit their missions. They all would've been dead a long time ago if it hadn't.

Riley blew out a breath. "We—I—plan to do that tomorrow." The colonel didn't need to know about Amy's involvement. "I figured the cops would be all over that beach tonight once the lifeguard reported the incident."

"Did she bring up your name?"

"She didn't have it," Riley lied smoothly. The colonel also didn't need to know he'd blabbed his name to Amy. If he bristled at the way Jack conducted himself, he'd pull out the little hair he had left over Riley's business model. "I'll get right on it and report back—when I have something to report."

As usual Colonel Scripps ended the call. Even though the team didn't report to the colonel in an official capacity anymore, the man was still in charge.

Riley ran the towel over his goose-pimpled flesh and hitched it around his waist. He rubbed his fist along the mirror to clear it. Then he plowed his fingers through his long hair, sluicing it back.

Wiping his hand against the towel snugly covering his backside, he poked his head into the living room. "You okay in here? How was the omelet?"

Perched on the stool at the counter, Amy tapped her empty plate. "Yummy, but I feel guilty. Come and eat your food before it gets any colder."

"Pop it in the microwave for a few seconds. I'm going to get dressed. A guy can only go commando for so long." He tugged at the towel.

"Go commando?"

"You know. No underwear." He grinned as Amy blushed. He knew he was playing with fire, but the heat felt so good.

He strolled into his bedroom and dressed quickly in shorts and a T-shirt. September in Southern California usually went out on a hot wave of summer heat—and the woman in his kitchen only made it hotter.

He sat down at the counter, and Amy placed a plate in front of him, steam curling from the yellow concoction. "Let me know if you want me to heat it up some more."

He wanted her to heat it up a lot more, but he didn't have food in mind. He sliced through the corner of his omelet with a fork and devoured it. "Mmm. That's fine."

She balanced on the edge of the stool next to him. "Can we talk now? Who was on the phone?"

"That was Colonel Frank Scripps. He pulled us all back together to find Jack and has all the right connections for this assignment."

She nodded encouragingly. "And what is this assignment?"

"I'm looking for my buddy, Jack Coburn." Riley sawed off another piece of egg.

"He's involved with this drug cartel or something?"

Riley slammed his fist on the counter. "No."

Amy's brows shot up. "Sorry. Touchy subject, huh?"

"I'd better start at the beginning." He ran his hands across his face. Where had it all begun? "I was a Navy SEAL serving in the Middle East. Colonel Scripps and a few other officers assembled a couple of special ops divisions to gather intelligence and generally work under the radar of military protocol."

"So you were a kind of spy?" The gold lights in Amy's dark eyes sparkled.

This woman liked living on the edge. "Don't look so excited. Our lives didn't exactly mimic a Robert Ludlum novel. This team of officers recruited me, Ian Dempsey from the U.S. Army Mountain Division, Buzz Richardson from the Air Force Special Ops Command, and the leader of Prospero, Jack Coburn, from the Office of Naval Intelligence."

"Prospero? Were you sorcerers like the character in Shakespeare's play?"

"Yeah, we pulled off a lot of magic." Riley shoved his plate away and planted his elbows on the counter. "Jack came up with the name. Usually he'd take a break from reading only long enough to round up terrorists."

A smile flitted across Amy's face. "He sounds…interesting. So you all retired from Prospero, except Jack, and now he's missing?"

"Even Jack retired from the military and Prospero, but instead of taking his hard-earned cash like the rest of us and kicking back, he took a job as a hostage nego-tiator. He disappeared while on a job in Afghanistan."

Amy shivered and clutched her arms. "That's a dangerous place. What does he have to do with the Velasquez Drug Cartel?"

"We don't know yet." Riley hunched his shoulders. "The Velasquez bunch was supposed to be getting a shipment of heroin from some terrorist organization with ties to Afghanistan. Jack's name came up in some chatter the CIA picked up. It's our first clue."

"A terrorist organization in Afghanistan? I can't believe Carlos Castillo was involved in all this." Shaking her head, she scooped up Riley's empty plate and stalked toward the sink.

Riley grabbed a glass of water and downed half of it. "I'm glad you brought up Carlos. It's my turn now. You met him on the beach and you two started dating?"

"That's pretty much it. You know as much as I do now." She cranked on the faucet and scrubbed the plate so hard Riley figured he might need a new plate before she finished.

He ran his knuckles across his stubble. "Carlos obviously targeted you for access to that beach, but why? Did he ever approach you about bringing a boat up on shore? Maybe he thought he could sweet talk you into looking the other way while his buddies picked up their shipment."

"That would take a ton of sugar, unless…" The plate cracked against the side of the sink. She held up the two pieces. "Sorry."

Riley hopped off the stool. "That's okay. Just be careful you don't cut yourself."

He took the plate from her and dropped the pieces

into the trash. "What were you going to say about Carlos?"

She slid the shiny forks into the dish drainer and turned, leaning her hips against the sink. "I forgot. Carlos probably just wanted info from me. He did ask a lot of questions about my job. He knew the beach would be deserted this time of year. He knew what time I got off work, and he probably knew it was my last shift today."

"But that still doesn't tell us what he was doing at your house." Riley crossed his arms over his chest.

"Maybe he wanted to warn me or make sure I was okay." She must have noticed the scowl twisting his face. "He wasn't a bad person, Riley."

"He was a drug dealer, Amy."

She reached over and toyed with the keys in the basket, making them jingle like wind chimes. "I know that. Sometimes criminals…people…do bad things, but they're still people. They have their good sides."

Riley cocked his head. He hadn't figured Amy for the bleeding-heart type, but she must've liked Carlos since she'd dated him.

Did she sleep with him, too? He dug his fingers into his biceps until it hurt. He didn't want to know the answer to that question.

"We need to check out the beach tomorrow. I want to get a good look at it during daylight. Will there be anyone there?"

"It's a weekday. No lifeguards on that beach anymore, and I think it's supposed to be overcast again." She cupped a set of keys in her palm. "Are these Carlos's keys?"

"Yeah. We should remove your house key from the

ring since I'm going to be leaving his car somewhere along with his keys."

Amy fiddled with the key chain, a crease forming between her brows. Then she gasped.

Riley's heart jumped. "What is it?"

Amy pinched a small gold key between her fingers, holding it aloft while the rest of the keys dangled below it. "I know what Carlos wanted on that beach."

Chapter Five

Riley lifted one brow and his gaze shifted from the key clutched between Amy's fingers to her eyes, bright and round above flushed cheeks.

"You do?"

"Yep." She jangled the keys that caught the recessed lighting and reflected in her eyes, giving them an added sparkle. "This is a distinctive key and it belongs to the storage unit on my beach."

"Storage unit?"

"We have a storage unit on that beach for buoys, extra equipment and supplies for the junior lifeguard program, which ended in the middle of the summer." She tossed the key chain to Riley, and he caught it with one hand.

He plucked out the gold key, with its squared-off end and dip in the middle. He hadn't wanted to involve Amy in any of this, but she'd jumped in with both feet and seemed to thrive on the thrill. Who was he to deny her?

"Would anyone else be in and out of this storage bin?"

"It's pretty much reserved for the junior lifeguards. When the program ends, nobody uses the storage until the following summer."

"A perfect drop location." Riley traced the edges of the unusual key with the tip of his finger. "Carlos got close to you to get access to the storage unit. He probably arranged for his contacts to leave the drugs in the storage unit, and the Velasquez Cartel was on its way to pick them up or scope out the location when we interrupted them."

Amy folded her arms on the counter and hunched over. "We interrupted them? I was in the lifeguard tower doing my job."

Riley grimaced. Just showed how much she'd become a part of the equation in his mind. "The diver was the scout to give the all clear for the boat to come up on the beach."

"Do you think they picked up the drugs?" She jerked upright and slapped the counter with her palms. "Maybe Carlos never left the drugs. Maybe that's why they killed him."

"I like the way you think, Amy. You ever consider a career in law enforcement?"

His teasing comment elicited bright red cheeks and a nervous laugh from her. "They wouldn't have me."

"I suppose it wouldn't do any good to suggest you stay here tomorrow while I search the beach?"

She shook her head and her ponytail whipped from side-to-side. "No. That's my beach. Besides—" she glanced over her shoulder at the kitchen window "—I don't want to be by myself."

Riley didn't want to leave her by herself either. "That's what I figured. Let's get some sleep. You can have the bedroom. I'll bunk out here on the couch."

"Are you sure?" Amy wrinkled her nose as she

peered around his shoulder at the small couch. "I think I'd fit more comfortably on the couch than you."

He shrugged. "I've slept on worse."

Riley dragged a blanket from the hall closet and tossed it onto his new bed while Amy slipped into the bedroom and shut the door. He brushed his teeth, and she stepped into the hallway clutching a pillow to her chest.

"Here's an extra pillow from the bed."

"Thanks."

He held out his arms, and she smashed the pillow against his chest and scurried into the bathroom. He caught a glimpse of her baggy nightshirt before she slammed the door. His brow furrowed. Why the modesty? She wasn't wearing anything from the pages of one of those sexy lingerie catalogs. Not that she needed to. Amy's natural beauty and feisty personality pushed all his buttons—including some he didn't even know he had.

He didn't figure he'd ever want to involve a woman in his business again, especially not after what had happened to April. But Amy wanted in, and not for the same reasons as April. Carlos Castillo had dragged Amy into his business, and she had a burning desire to finish it.

Riley dropped his shorts by the edge of the couch and peeled off his T-shirt. He punched the pillow a few times and dragged the blanket over his shoulders.

The bathroom door clicked open, a shaft of light slicing across the hall.

Amy poked her head into the living room. "Are you okay? There's still time to switch."

"I'm good." He waved his arm, the blanket slipping from his shoulder. "Go ahead and make yourself comfortable in my bed."

Without me.

Amy hesitated, a soft sigh escaping from her lips. Riley held his breath. Was she about to issue an invitation?

"Th-thanks, Riley. Good night."

Riley eased back against the cushion. Of course she wouldn't ask him to join her. They'd just met. Today. On the beach. Under fire. They barely knew each other.

AMY PEELED OPEN ONE EYELID and focused on the sunlight sifting through the blinds. After thrashing around and twisting the bedcovers into a hopeless knot, she welcomed the morning after the sleepless night she'd spent in Riley's bed.

Replaying the previous day's events in her mind had kept her wide-awake, wide-eyed and fearful. Once she'd talked herself back away from the ledge, her thoughts scrambled down another just-as-torturous path—Riley Hammond half-naked in the other room.

For one crazy moment last night, she'd almost suggested he join her in bed. The lust factor did play a role in her almost-invitation, but she also craved a warm body for comfort. Those old familiar feelings of loneliness had washed over her when she'd slipped between the cool sheets of Riley's bed alone.

She snorted and buried her face in the pillow. As if Riley would've been interested in cuddling away her fears all night. That wouldn't have even been enough for her. Once she got her hands on his rock-hard bod...

The rap on the bedroom door had her yanking the covers to her chin. She cleared her throat. "Yes?"

The door cracked open a sliver.

"You're awake? I didn't want to disturb you before, but we should get going."

She gasped and shot upright. "Is it late?"

"About ten o'clock." He pushed open the door and wedged a shoulder against the doorjamb, his long hair wet and slicked back from his face. "We had a late night, and you needed your sleep."

She rubbed her eyes. She still needed her sleep. It figured. She'd dozed off at the break of dawn and slept in.

Scrambling from the bed, she said, "Looks like you already showered. You probably need to get in here and get dressed."

Pulling her oversize T-shirt past her thighs, Amy's gaze tracked across Riley's bare chest. She worked on the beach and all the male lifeguards she knew spent half their time shirtless, but the sight of Riley's flat planes of muscle and ridged abs left her breathless.

His blue eyes darkened as he crossed his arms over those amazing pecs. Had she unsettled him with her unabashed appreciation of his male assets?

He cocked one brow and a lazy smile played across his lips as his muscles seemed to bunch up even more.

Unsettled? Hardly.

Amy turned and dipped her head into her suitcase. "I'll grab some clothes and hit the shower."

She pawed through a jumble of shorts and T-shirts. What did one wear on a spying mission? Wrapping her arms around a bundle of clothes, she headed for the door where Riley's solid frame loomed in the opening.

He stepped aside, and she brushed past him, her arm skimming his.

"How'd you sleep?"

His voice so close to her ear made her jump. "Huh?"

"How'd you sleep? No bumps in the night?"

"Plenty, but they were all in my head." She stumbled into the bathroom, still misty from Riley's shower. She inhaled the steam and savored the scent of masculinity that whispered on the air.

She shook her head. Maybe she should adjust the water temperature to freezing to quell these fantasies about Riley. After her lukewarm shower, she toweled off and pulled on a pair of shorts and a T-shirt. Then she padded to the living room.

Riley, dressed in jeans and a black tee, sat hunched over the counter, nursing a cup of coffee and scanning a newspaper.

He glanced up when she walked into the room. "Do you want some bran flakes or instant oatmeal?"

"I'll take the cold cereal." She plopped down on the stool across from him and reached for the box of bran flakes. "Anything in that paper about last night's activities?"

"Nope. I guess you weren't that convincing." He collected a bowl and a spoon from the dish drainer on the sink and shoved them across to her.

"I wouldn't trust those cops to find a lollipop in a candy store anyway."

Riley blinked and studied her face.

Tone down the vehemence about the police, girl. Amy ignored his puzzled gaze and dumped some cereal in her bowl. Riley got the hint and retreated to his bedroom where he proceeded to bang closet doors and drawers. She hoped he'd emerge with some tools of his trade— guns, knives, grenades.

Riley joined her in the kitchen with a promising black bag slung over one shoulder. He scooped up Carlos's keychain and swung it around his finger. "Are you ready to investigate?"

Amy dropped her dishes in the sink. "I'm as ready as I'll ever be, but what happens if we don't find anything? What next?"

"I search for new leads, and you watch your back."

Amy shivered and clenched her teeth. She didn't like the sound of that proposition at all.

A half hour later, Riley pulled Carlos's car into the almost deserted beach parking lot. With summer over and school back in session, only a few die-hard runners and walkers occupied the barren sands. Surfers found better waves up the coast and fishermen had the pier farther north for their activities.

As he rolled past the empty spaces, Riley asked, "Where's the storage container?"

"South end of the beach. Just over that rise. You can't see it from the parking lot."

Perfect place to stash some illegal contraband. Riley nabbed the last space on the south side of the lot and grabbed his black bag out of the trunk.

Amy pointed to the bag as Riley hitched it over his shoulder. "What's in there?"

"A few necessities of life."

"Bet your necessities are a lot different from mine."

"If you hang out with me long enough, you'll come to appreciate mine more."

She wouldn't mind giving it a try. Amy clumped across the dry sand next to Riley. But back at his place he'd made it pretty clear that if they hit a dead end on the beach, she'd be on her own, Looking over her shoulder.

Not that she was any stranger to looking over her shoulder. Or being on her own.

They traipsed up a small dune and the storage unit rose from the sand, an ominous dark gray shape. Amy shoved her hands in her pockets to hide their slight trembling. She'd never considered the junior lifeguard shed scary before.

"Do you want to do the honors?" Riley dragged the keys from his front pocket and dangled them from one finger.

Amy held out her hand, and Riley dropped them into her palm. She selected the unusual key from the ring and lifted the lock securing the door. With shaky fingers, she tried to insert the key into the lock, finding success on her third try.

Riley helped her pull open the heavy door, which creaked on rusty hinges. Amy sniffed at the briny scent that lived in every corner of the storage unit.

As her gaze tracked across the cleared-out space in the center of the unit, her breath hitched, and she grabbed the edge of the door.

"What's wrong?" Riley hovered over her left shoulder.

"This." She swept one arm in front of her. "We didn't leave it like this."

"You mean this clearing?" Riley stepped around her and parked in the middle of the circle ringed with buoys, life vests, surfboards and paddle boards.

"We stacked all this equipment at the end of the junior guard session. Someone's pushed it out of the way to make room for…" Amy hugged herself, suddenly cold in the stuffy unit.

Riley crouched beside her, running his hands over the cement flooring just beyond the shaft of light from the open door. He turned his hands over and studied his palms, as if trying to read his future.

"Do you see anything?" Amy leaned over his shoulder and peered at the sand and grit stuck to his palms.

"No." He brushed his hands together. "But then I didn't expect them to leave any heroin behind."

"W-what would it look like?" Her gaze darted around the storage facility.

"Probably a brown powder or a black tar form. The couriers from Afghanistan might have already packaged it in balloons for Velasquez to sell on the street." Riley braced his hands on his knees. "But I think it's clear Carlos made this space available to the dealers from Afghanistan to leave their delivery for the Velasquez Cartel."

Amy squatted next to him, wrapping her arms around her knees. "And Velasquez's boys picked it up last night. That's why they didn't come after us after those initial shots. They found what they came for. That could've been the end of it."

"Except for Carlos." Riley brushed a wisp of hair from her cheek. "They came after Carlos because they didn't trust him or because he didn't deliver the money for the shipment."

"That still doesn't get us beyond square one. Why did Carlos return to my house? I just don't—"

"Shh." Riley sliced a hand across his throat.

Amy covered her mouth with her hand as a shadow

passed by the open door to the unit, momentarily blocking the sun that had given them their only light.

Jumping to his feet, Riley pulled the gun from his waistband. Amy toppled sideways into the paddle boards. *How'd he whip that out so fast?* She hadn't even realized he'd been packing anything other than the stash in the black bag.

Clutching the weapon in his right hand, Riley crept toward the door and poked his head outside. He called over his shoulder, "You saw that, right?"

"I saw a darkening at the door, but it could've been a cloud moving over the sun, or a bird."

"That's one helluva bird to blot out the sun."

"Do you see anything?"

"Just a couple walking in the distance, but these dunes make it hard to see for any distance." He spun around, tucking the gun back into his waistband. "Let's get out of here and take a look at the lifeguard tower."

Amy scrambled to her knees and gripped the thick edges of the paddle board, shoving it back against the others. A sliver of silver glinted behind the board. Amy's fingers inched along the gritty floor and she slid the hard, smooth object toward her.

She pinched her find between two fingers and shifted into the light, holding it up for inspection. Her heart slammed against her rib cage.

"What's that?" Riley knelt beside her.

Amy opened her mouth, emitted tiny gasps of air. Squeezing her eyes shut, she shook her head and scooped in a deep breath.

Don't be ridiculous, Amy. Dad's in prison.

"It's a cigarette holder." She held the slim tube flattened on one end under Riley's nose, her fingers covering the initials engraved on the end.

"You don't see many of those around anymore." He plucked the holder from her fingers and pushed to his feet. In two steps he reached the square of sunlight and examined the holder. "I suppose none of the lifeguards smoke or happen to use a cigarette holder?"

Feeling like she had just aged twenty years, Amy staggered to her feet and stretched. "None of the lifeguards smoke, and I've never seen any of them use a cigarette holder."

"What about Carlos?"

"Not a smoker."

"And his initials aren't E.P." Riley rubbed the pad of his thumb along the edge of the cigarette holder.

"Initials?" Amy clenched her jaw and swallowed hard.

"Engraved on the side." Riley tossed the object into the air and caught it, closing his fist around it. "Looks like we have a piece of evidence."

"I don't see what good some anonymous cigarette holder is going to do us." Amy pushed the hair out of her face and stalked past Riley. Once outside, she gulped in the fresh sea air.

The hinges of the storage unit protested as Riley swung the door shut with a bang. "You never know. Any evidence is better than none. Are you okay?"

"Yeah." She spun around and heaved against the heavy door with her shoulder as Riley secured the lock.

He snapped the lock into place and cocked his head. "You look pale. I mean, beneath your suntan, which is even weirder."

"I was getting creeped out in there." She wiped the back of her hand across her mouth, relieved the trembling had stopped. "I'm half Mexican, you know. I tan easily."

Riley wedged a finger beneath her chin and tilted. "Is that where the pretty, dark eyes come from and the dark hair with the auburn sheen to it? Your mother must be Mexican. Is Prescott English?"

Amy slipped from his inspection, a swath of that dark hair with the auburn sheen hiding her hot face. Had he really noticed that much about her?

"I guess, just a mishmash of American mutt." *With an emphasis on mutt.* "Hey, can we check out the rest of the beach now?"

He paused for a few seconds and then pocketed the key and the cigarette holder. "Let's go."

Amy shuffled behind Riley, twisting her hands in front of her. She really didn't want to go into her family lineage with him. After discovering her background, he just might suspect her entire involvement in this mess.

They searched the area near the water where Velasquez's man died. Then they poked around the lifeguard tower, which Amy had locked up last night when she'd returned with the sheriff's deputies.

Riley grabbed the base of the tower and leaned forward, the muscles in his back and shoulders a rippled outline beneath his T-shirt. "Did you ever find your wallet?"

"Right here where I dropped it." Amy pointed her toe at the sand beneath the tower. "So if the guys from the boat did use it to get my address, they left it behind."

Dropping his lashes over his blue eyes, Riley mumbled, "I don't think they needed your wallet, Amy."

"You think they already had my address?" She licked her lips, tasting the salt from the moist air. "Carlos must've told them about me. But how did they know to find Carlos at my place?"

"They either followed him or staked out your house."

"Riley." Amy burrowed the toes of her tennis shoes into the dry sand. "If the Velasquez goons or their customers already killed Carlos and picked up their drugs from the storage unit, what did they want from me last night? Why'd they return?"

Riley spread his hands, sand clinging to his palms and fingers, and lifted his shoulders. Strong shoulders. Capable hands. A man you could trust. Maybe.

"Let's put a positive spin on this." He shifted his gaze to the ocean, his eyes reflecting the grayish-blue water.

"I'm ready for positive."

"Carlos double-crossed both parties, so they were both after him. Someone got lucky and nailed him first. The other party was still after him last night, and maybe now they know he's dead. If so, your involvement ends there."

"I like the sound of that. I'll stay with my friends for a few days to be on the safe side, and then I'm going to try to put this behind me."

His eyes widened. "You can do that?"

Riley had no idea how much she'd already put behind her. What was one murdered, drug-dealing ex-boyfriend? As she watched the sea breeze toss the ends of Riley's sun-washed hair, Amy swallowed. Putting Riley behind her was a whole other matter.

"I had already forgotten about Carlos. Now it'll just be easier."

Riley whistled. "Ooh, that's cold. Okay, I'm just going to have to be satisfied with my cigarette holder. Maybe it will lead me to someone or something."

Amy opened her mouth and then snapped it shut. The fact that her father used a cigarette holder would be of no interest to Riley. Her father had nothing to do with the events of the past twenty-four hours.

"Are you ready?" Riley grabbed her hand, the grit from his fingers grating across her skin.

She left her hand in his, wondering if the buzz she felt at their connection would dull to a hum. She had to steel herself to walk away from this man. She was probably mistaking the adrenaline rush for attraction.

He opened the car door for her and she slid onto the warm leather seat and closed her eyes. She didn't need the excitement. She didn't want the excitement. She could have a typical relationship with a normal, boring guy. Women did it every day.

Riley dropped onto the driver's seat and blew out a breath. "I'd call this a productive outing."

"You would? Finding a random cigarette holder is productive?"

He pulled it out of his pocket and held it up to the windshield. "It's unusual. It has the owner's initials. I have a few contacts with the Velasquez Cartel. It should be easy to track down the owner."

Amy tucked her hands beneath her thighs. She just hoped the owner had nothing to do with her father. "I'll leave the spy work to you. I'll grab my stuff from your place and drop in on my friends. They left me a text message on my cell."

Cranking on the engine, Riley slanted a cool gaze her way. "Are you sure you're going to be okay?"

"I have to go back to my normal life at some point." Amy clicked her seat belt and powered down the window. She needed air.

Riley wheeled out of the parking lot, the sand crunching beneath the tires. He pulled onto the street and idled at the first red light, glancing into his rearview mirror.

His gaze wandered back to the mirror and then he checked his side mirror. His hands tensed on the steering wheel.

Amy's pulse ratcheted up several notches as an engine roared behind them. She checked the mirror on the passenger side and gripped the armrest. A black SUV was barreling toward them. She braced her feet against the floor of the car, waiting for the impact. "What the…?"

Riley cursed and punched the accelerator. "The guy's coming right for us. And he's not going to stop."

Chapter Six

Riley gripped the steering wheel, held his breath and flew through the intersection, narrowly avoiding a minivan. Amy squealed beside him, jerking forward against her suddenly taut seat belt.

The BMW hugged the road while Riley eased off the gas pedal. He checked his mirror again. The black SUV careened through the intersection against the light and lunged toward them.

"Hold on," Riley shouted. He grasped the leather-wrapped wheel and turned sharply, taking the corner at high speed and giving silent thanks to Carlos for his high-performance car.

The SUV lumbered after them, squealing around the corner with purpose. A sick feeling lodged in Riley's belly as the yellow school-crossing signs flashed ahead.

Thank God the streets remained empty. School must still be in session. He sped through the crosswalk just slow enough to see the crossing guard's mouth drop open. The SUV followed in his path, knocking over the sign with the yellow flashing lights.

From his mirror, Riley saw the crossing guard

shake her fist and reach inside her vest. *That's right, sweetheart. Call the cops.*

He couldn't afford to be pulled over in a car that belonged to a dead man, but the inhabitants of that black SUV would have a lot of explaining to do, too. He wouldn't be surprised if the cops found a few outstanding warrants in that car.

Velasquez always employed punks to do his dirty work.

Riley took the next turn, and Amy fell against his shoulder. "How you doing, beach girl?"

She hunched over to look in the passenger mirror. "That's them isn't it? That's Velasquez."

"I don't know who else would be chasing us around town." Riley planned to avoid the freeway—too much visibility. He could lose them faster in the side streets, and he knew just the area.

Imperial Beach was always a little more working class than its glittery neighbors, Coronado and La Jolla. And it had the warehouses to prove it.

Riley let the Beemer do its thing as he peeled out, reaching almost a hundred down a straight shot toward a collection of silver-and-dun-colored warehouse buildings. Trucks trundled in and around the buildings, delivering goods from the harbor.

"Where are you heading? We're going to get cornered."

"Do you think those thugs are going to try anything with a bunch of truckers around? Besides, I have a plan. I always have a plan."

The car hummed as Riley maneuvered it through two parking lots. He'd left the SUV in the dust a half mile ago. Would the driver have the *cojones* to follow him into this maze of buildings?

A warehouse door gaped open in front of Riley, and he zoomed into the building, pulling the car to the side.

Amy swiveled her head around. "Are you going to hide in here?"

"Why not?"

"That's why." She jerked her thumb toward the back window where a couple of the warehouse workers started to amble their way.

"They're not going to bother a couple looking for a little privacy." He reached across the console, wrapped one hand behind her neck and pulled her close.

Amy's eyelids fluttered shut as she braced a hand against his chest. His heart thundered beneath her light touch. He weaved his fingers through the hair at the nape of her neck and brushed her lips with his.

They panted against each other's mouths. The adrenaline continued to rush through Riley's veins at warp speed. He couldn't distinguish between the thrill of the chase and the passion that pounded in his blood.

Ah, hell. Sometimes they were one and the same.

He possessed Amy's sweet lips in a kiss so pure, it made his teeth ache. Chaste. Make-believe. At least that's what he wanted her to think.

She turned her head so that his lips ended up somewhere on her jaw. She sighed. He cupped her face for a repeat performance. She laughed.

"It worked."

"Huh?"

"Not only did our nosy, blue-collar workers back off,

but we outmaneuvered the SUV. They won't find us here."

Disappointment speared his gut. "They could still be lurking around."

"I don't think so." She twisted in her seat. "I guess that positive scenario you dreamed up is just that. A dream. They want me for something."

"Or they want *me* for something."

She clasped her hands between her knees. "Then maybe we'd better split up and find out who they prefer."

Riley's breathing slowed down and he regained partial use of his brain. He wanted to keep Amy with him to protect her, but maybe the threat of danger hung over his head and not hers. In which case, her proximity to him would endanger her, not protect her.

It all had a familiar ring.

He had to cut her loose and allow her to get back to her life. There didn't appear to be any logical reason why the Velasquez Cartel would be interested in Amy. She couldn't identify even one of them. She'd demonstrated that in her report to the police. The police who didn't believe a word of her story. They had to know that by now, had to know she didn't pose any threat to them at all.

"You're probably right. I don't want to endanger you any more than I already have." Riley buzzed down the window and gulped diesel-scented air.

"You didn't endanger me, Riley. That was Carlos."

"I'm not making your life any easier." He turned over the engine and rolled out the other side of the warehouse, poking the nose of the car into the parking lot. He scanned the area, ignoring the grins of the warehouse workers. No sign of the black SUV.

"I'll take you back to my place and you can grab your stuff and I'll drop you off at your car. I still think you should hang out with your friends for a day or two."

"I will." She tapped her purse. "My friend left me that text message. I'll let her know I'm on my way over."

Blowing out a breath, Riley sped toward the highway. He had to get rid of this car now that Velasquez's guys had it on their radar.

Twenty minutes later he pulled into the parking garage of his apartment building. His hands tightened briefly on the steering wheel as Amy exited the car. Every nerve fiber in his body protested at letting her go, but she had a life to live. She couldn't spend it running around with him chasing bad guys.

He made a habit out of pursuing bad guys. For Amy, this incident would be a blip in her calm life. Something to tell the grandkids about.

His feet felt like lead as he tromped down the hallway toward the elevator behind her. They rode in silence, staring at the lighted numbers like a couple of strangers.

She leaned against the outside wall while he fumbled for his keys. He asked, "Do you want something to eat before you head over to your friends' place?"

"I don't want to be a bother to you anymore."

Riley shrugged, trying hard to mimic a nonchalance that he didn't feel. *Let her go. Keep her safe.*

They entered the apartment and Amy propped a hip against the counter, texting on her phone, the little beeps as she entered each letter reverberating in his head like a death knell.

He really did have control issues. He passed a hand across his face and grabbed a glass from the cupboard. "Water?"

She looked up from her phone and hit one final button. "Sure. High-speed car chases really make me thirsty."

"I'm sorry."

"Stop—" she sliced her hand through the air "—apologizing. It's not your fault, Riley. You saved my life on more than one occasion. I trusted the right guy last night."

And now he had to honor that trust and get her clear of this madness. "I'll get your bag."

She trailed after him, the sweet smell of her hair giving him all sorts of crazy ideas. She made a detour into the bathroom and collected her things while he wheeled her suitcase into the living room next to the door.

"I guess that's everything." She stuffed her toiletry bag into the side compartment of the suitcase.

"Did you hear back from your friends yet?" He gestured toward the cell phone clutched in her right hand.

"Not yet, but they'll come through. They always do. I just sent a text that I was on my way."

"Let's get you back to your car."

Amy ambled down the corridor, moving at half-speed. Could she be feeling the same reluctance as he felt?

Riley kept conversation to a minimum on the ride back to Amy's place. What more could he say? He pulled up behind her car and grabbed her bag from Carlos's Beemer.

She popped her trunk, and he hoisted the suitcase inside and slammed it shut for her. He rested his hand on the driver's door handle. "I know you told me to stop apologizing, but I need to go there once more."

Amy shook her head and a swath of dark hair swept over her shoulder. "I think you already hit your apology quota."

"The kiss." He blurted it out like a pimply faced teen. What had happened to his smooth lines? He swung open her door. "One of the many tricks of the trade."

He gritted his teeth behind his stupid grin. Now he sounded like a seventies' disco dude.

Amy raised her brows. "Okay, whatever. It wasn't a big deal."

Now his grin was hurting his face. *Not a big deal?* "Right. I just wanted to make it look good for the guys in the warehouse. No big deal."

She stuck out her hand. "Thanks for sticking with me. I'm pretty sure I would've fallen apart without your support."

Riley narrowed his eyes. He seriously doubted that. Taking her hand, he swirled his thumb along her inner wrist. "Be careful, beach girl. You have my cell phone number in there. Use it if you need help."

"Will do." She slipped her hand from his and ducked into the car.

As she pulled away from the curb, he smacked the trunk of the car and waved. He'd cursed his bad luck when Amy came running into the ocean to save him.

Now as he watched her take the turn and disappear, he felt as if a vital organ had just been ripped from his chest.

AMY BLINKED AWAY TEARS as she watched Riley's blurry form in her rearview mirror. She dashed a hand across her eyes. *Buck up, girl. You operate better on your own anyway. Always have.*

She planned to put this little bump on the road to a normal, sedate life firmly behind her. No more married men. No more drug dealers. No more secret agents. She giggled at her list. Most women wouldn't even dream of making a list like that.

Most women didn't have Elijah Prescott for a father.

Amy's cell phone buzzed and she groped for it in her purse. She checked the display and let out a noisy sigh. "Hi, Sarah."

"Amy? Are you okay? Your message was weird."

Weird? Amy had a few other choice words about her predicament. "You don't know the half of it, and I don't have the energy to explain it. Can I crash at your place for a few days? I'll even babysit for free."

"Of course, you can stay here but we're leaving tonight for Florida. Cliff's mom had another fall. She's not doing well, so we're taking the kids back for a visit. It might be their last."

"Sorry to hear that. I can house-sit for you."

"Is it Carlos?"

Amy caught her breath. "What?"

"Is Carlos calling you again? Don't go back to him, Amy. That's a dead end."

Oh, boy. Sarah had never spoken truer words. "Going back to Carlos is an impossibility at this point."

"I'm glad to hear you say that, even though I never suspected for a minute you'd take him back. There's a new attorney at Cliff's firm. Maybe we can all get together for dinner some night."

Amy drew in a quick breath. If he didn't have deep blue eyes, a boyish grin, a fondness for knives and a penchant for engaging in high-speed chases, she'd have to pass.

"Maybe. I'm on my way to your place right now. Is that okay, or are you too busy packing for Florida?"

"We're done packing. You can join us for dinner and then save us taxi fare to the airport by giving us a ride."

"Sounds like a deal."

Amy ended the call and dropped her cell phone into the cup holder. She could always count on Sarah. Sarah had been like a big sister to her when she'd volunteered at Amy's middle school to tutor at-risk kids. Sarah was the one who had gotten Amy involved in the San Diego County Junior Lifeguard program.

Sarah had saved her life.

When Amy arrived at the house, she busied herself playing with the kids and avoided Sarah's worried, questioning glances. Her face must have had Major Stress written all over it.

When Cliff took the kids with him to pick up their dinner from the neighborhood Chinese restaurant, Sarah planted herself in front of Amy and placed her hands on Amy's shoulders.

"What happened to you? You're jumpier than one of the girls' Mexican jumping beans."

Amy's shoulders sagged beneath Sarah's light touch. She never could keep anything from her. Didn't want to.

As Amy recounted the previous day's adventures and today's car chase, Sarah's soft doe eyes grew rounder and bigger.

"How do you know you can trust this Riley character?"

"Sarah, he saved my life more than once in the past twenty-four hours. I can trust him." Amy dropped her lashes. "Besides, he's moved on anyway. I doubt I'll ever see him again."

"That's a good thing, Amy. You need to extricate yourself from this situation, pronto." She rubbed Amy's shoulder. "Stay here while we're gone. Are you done with lifeguarding right now?"

"Yeah, yesterday was my last shift. That tower closes until next summer."

"When does EMT School start?"

"In two weeks, and then I might start applying to fire departments."

"You can do whatever you set out to do. I've seen it." Sarah jerked her head toward the front door as Cliff staggered into the room carrying a daughter in one arm and bags of take-out food in the other.

Amy put her finger to her lips, and Sarah rolled her eyes. Amy knew Sarah would tell her husband everything, but probably not until they reached thirty thousand feet. That's how far away Amy needed Cliff to be to avoid his interference. He'd taken on the role of big brother, always eager to pick up any cause of Sarah's.

Amy stashed her worries in the corner as she helped Sarah's daughters navigate their food with chopsticks. Their squeals and giggles washed over her in a soothing balm.

This glimpse into Sarah's family life always created a small ache in the pit of her belly. But it made her more determined to find that for herself—if she could only banish one blue-eyed adventurer from her mind.

While the girls brushed their teeth, Amy grabbed the dinner plates and stacked them in the sink. She waved off Sarah. "Go help the girls get ready. I'll clean up when I come back from dropping you off at the airport."

The family bustled out of the house, and Amy took their minivan to drop them off. When she arrived back at the house, she double-checked the locks on the doors and windows. Couldn't be too safe when you had drug dealers on your trail.

Maybe now those drug dealers had just one trail to follow—Riley's. A sprinkling of goose bumps raced up her arms, even though if anyone knew how to take care of himself, Riley did. He knew how to take care of her too.

Enough. She smacked her hands together, the sound echoing through the silent house. And enough of this hand-wringing over her fate or, worse, leaving it to Riley to sort out. When did she ever wait for someone else to take action?

She dumped out the contents of her purse and snatched her cell phone. She scrolled through her contacts and selected the one she dreaded the most. Placing the call, she paced the length of the family room, avoiding doll houses and a railroad track.

She held her breath as the man on the other end answered the phone. "San Miguel Federal Penitentiary."

Chapter Seven

Amy Prescott was a liar.

Riley ran his finger along the smooth cigarette holder and then tapped it against his palm. Amy knew something about this holder and for some reason had decided to keep that information to herself.

He should've figured this seemingly innocent bystander had secrets. Maybe Carlos hadn't been an ex-boyfriend but a current one, and Amy was not only his lover but his partner in crime.

Which made the kiss in the car even dumber. The thought left a sour taste in his mouth, and he took another gulp of coffee to wash it away. Amy should've realized you never lie to a liar.

His cell phone vibrated and he slid it open. "Do you have something for me, Chet?"

Chet whistled. "You have yourself a doozy. I sure hope this is professional and not personal because you need to stay far, far away from this girl."

Riley clenched his gut as if expecting a blow to the midsection. So Amy had played him all along. "Professional. Go ahead."

"Do you remember Eli Prescott?"

Riley dug his fingers into the arm of his chair. This was gonna be bad. "No."

Chet snorted. "Yeah, I guess you're a young 'un. Before your time."

"Well?" Riley gritted his teeth. Chet Bennett, the seasoned CIA agent always had to lord his knowledge over the younger guys. Riley hated owing the man favors, but Chet could conjure up information with the snap of his fingers.

"Elijah Benjamin Prescott was a militia-style survivalist in Idaho. When things got too hot in the States, he high-tailed it to Mexico and set up shop there. The Mexican government didn't mind too much until old Eli started making deals with some of the drug lords. Then the Mexican government decided to cooperate with the FBI, and the two agencies raided the compound."

"Amy Prescott is related to this man?" Riley hoped the words came out casually despite his dry throat.

"Amy Prescott is his daughter."

Riley grunted, his fingers almost drilling holes in the fabric of the chair. So Amy and Carlos had had a deal with the Velazquez Cartel, and the situation had gotten a little too hot to handle. She had used him to get away.

"It gets better."

At the sound of Chet's smug voice, Riley wanted to punch him. He wanted to punch someone or something.

"Your Amy was at the compound when the fibbies raided it. Eli had no intention of going down without a fight. Amy's Mexican-born mother was killed during the raid, and her father was arrested."

Riley's anger shifted from Amy to the clods who

had raided the compound. Amy must have been a child when this happened. "When did this all go down?"

"Let's see." Chet clicked a few keys. "The raid occurred over fifteen years ago."

"What happened to Amy?"

"Relatives took in the kids if they wanted them, but Amy's relatives didn't want anything to do with crazy Eli's spawn. She went into the system."

No surprise Amy didn't trust law enforcement. "Kids? Amy has siblings?"

"I guess. But it would take a geneticist to figure out the familial relationships at the compound. Eli had multiple wives. Amy's mother was just one of three or four."

Riley satisfied himself by punching the cushion next to him. What Amy went through didn't justify illegal activity, but she'd had a helluva time growing up.

"If you like, I have a picture I can send you of Eli with his very extended family."

"Sure." Riley rattled off his email address. "Is Eli still alive?"

"He's at the San Miguel FCI. He'll never get out though."

Riley thanked Chet for the information and ended the call. He sprang from the chair and buried his fingers in his hair as he wandered toward the window.

Just because Amy had a criminal, drug-dealing father didn't necessarily mean she'd cooperated with a criminal, drug-dealing boyfriend. Could all be just some weird cosmic coincidence.

He powered up his laptop on the coffee table and accessed his email. Chet's message scrolled by, and Riley opened it and clicked on the attachment.

The picture filled his screen—a tall man, holding a long cigarette, with his hair pulled back in a ponytail standing among a group of women and children. Riley counted four women and nine children.

He peered closely at the screen, running his finger along the faces of the children. It hovered over the smiling face of a young girl with long brown hair, long legs and dirty bare feet. Had to be Amy.

He skimmed over the remaining children. Amy looked about ten years old in this picture. Some of the other children were younger, and some looked to be in their teens.

Riley shifted his attention back to Eli Prescott and squinted at the long cigarette he held in his hand. Why was it so long? Looked like the ones FDR used to smoke.

His pulse ticked in his jaw while he reached for the cigarette holder. He saved the picture to his computer and opened it with a photo editor. Then he zoomed in on the object Prescott held carelessly in his right hand while his left rested on top of a child's head.

Eli Prescott had a cigarette holder—one exactly like the one Riley cradled in the palm of his hand. A weird cosmic coincidence?

THE FOLLOWING MORNING, Amy raced up the 805 freeway with the cool air-conditioning blowing on her face. She'd made this journey before and had never found what she was looking for. She didn't know what to expect this time. Maybe some answers.

She pulled up to the gate of the San Miguel Federal Penitentiary and handed over her driver's license. The guard at the gate held it pinched between two fingers, as if he feared contamination, and tipped his dark sunglasses down on his nose.

He muttered, "Prescott."

Amy met his gaze with an unflinching one of her own. If he wanted to tar her with the same brush as her infamous father, it wouldn't be the first time. Wouldn't be the last.

She narrowed her eyes. "You done checking out the freak?"

He shrugged and handed back the license. She snatched it from his fingers and tossed it onto the passenger seat as she accelerated through the gate toward the gray buildings.

A red balloon sailed over the barbwire gates, incongruous against the drab backdrop of the prison. Amy tracked it until she lost it over the line of trees. Had one of the inmates had a birthday party?

The pen had an administrative building outside the main prison gates, but Amy had never been inside. Her visits took place in the bowels of the prison. No balloons there.

After running the security gauntlet, Amy perched on the edge of a plastic chair in the visiting room. She jumped each time the door behind the glass panel buzzed.

On the fourth buzz, a tall, lean man with close-cropped gray hair shuffled into the room behind the barrier. As his blue gaze alighted on Amy, a wide smile split his craggy face.

Amy scooted her chair closer to the glass as the guard led her father to an opposing chair. With a hammering heart, she picked up the red receiver first and waited while Dad settled into his seat, his movements stiff and jerky.

"Hello, Amy. It's been a while."

"Hey, Dad."

"You look good, healthy. Tall like me and pretty like your mother."

He remembered which child belonged with which mother? Oh, yeah. Her mother was special. She's the one the Feds murdered. She pursed her lips. She never talked back to her father. The man scared her—always had.

"You look…different."

His hacking laugh turned into a cough, and the guard brought him a cup of water.

"You mean old."

Amy didn't refute him. The tall, vigorous man who had controlled his cult with an iron fist now walked with a shuffle and stoop. His hair, once pulled back into his trademark ponytail, now lay like a gray cap close to his skull.

She lifted a shoulder. "Different."

"What brings you here? Of all my children, I believe you resent me the most. Of course, you were Loretta's only child, and she babied you a bit. I know her death hit you hard. You shouldn't blame me, Amy. Put the blame on those hot-headed FBI agents."

For once she didn't come here to relive the past, to get answers as to why he seriously messed up her childhood. The present concerned her now. The present and that silver cigarette holder in the storage bin.

She waved her hand at the glass as if to dispel the image there. "Are you involved in any illegal activity on the outside?"

His tired blue eyes brightened as he shifted his gaze toward the guard. "Why do you ask? I'm in here paying my debt to society—no more, no less."

"Do you still use those silver cigarette holders with your initials?"

"In here?" He shook his head. "I still smoke, but they wouldn't allow me to have a cigarette holder inside. You remember those, huh?"

"I just saw one yesterday, and it had an *E* and a *P* engraved on it."

His gaze narrowed and he hunched forward. Amy automatically shifted away from the glass. She could feel his presence emanating from behind the glass like a snake preparing to strike.

He whispered into the phone. "You saw a silver cigarette holder with my initials?"

Amy nodded and swallowed hard as her childhood fears assailed her once again. Maybe this wasn't such a great idea.

"Where?" The word came out like a breath of chilly air. She almost expected the glass to ice over and crack.

"Let's just say it was at the scene of a crime."

"Someone probably copying my style. Why do you care?" He shifted back in his chair, crossing an ankle over his knee.

"I care because that someone got me involved in a dangerous situation, and I want to know who and why."

"You didn't really think I'd made an escape from my current digs, did you? Even I can't manage that."

"Of course not, but maybe you know someone who

might have a cigarette holder with your initials, someone who would want to copy your style."

"Maybe you should've kept in touch with your half siblings over the years, Amy."

"What does that mean?"

"Leave it alone, girl." He settled the receiver in its cradle and pushed back from the table.

Amy dug the phone against her ear as her father held out his wrists for the cuffs and slipped through the door, escaping her questions once again.

She banged the receiver into the cradle a couple of times, and then slumped forward, resting her forehead against the glass. Did she really believe she'd get anything out of the man? Apparently, the FBI hadn't gotten much out of him after his arrest. What chance did she have?

Sighing, she stumbled to her feet and pressed the call button next to the door. After a loud click, the guard in the hallway swung open the door, and she followed his ramrod back in his pressed khaki shirt down the long corridor.

She shoved her hands into the pockets of her billowing skirt and filled her lungs with fresh air, blinking in the radiant sunlight. The squeals of the children in the picnic area near the administration building conjured images of just another day in the park, but the barbed wire and armed guards told a different story.

Would these children return here as adults seeking answers to unfathomable questions? Would they walk away empty?

The gravel crunched beneath her flats as she walked toward the parking lot. Engrossed in her own pathetic musings, she nearly collided with a tall man in black slacks and a snowy-white shirt.

"Making your escape?"

She jerked up her head and choked. "Riley!"

"Quick, I'll drive the getaway car."

"What are you doing here?" Amy rubbed her eyes as if she couldn't believe the vision shimmering before her in the desert heat—Riley, all six-foot-something of him decked out in sharp black slacks, a white dress shirt tucked neatly into the pants, emphasizing the trim waist flaring into a set of broad shoulders.

He cleaned up nicely—damned nicely.

She wedged her hands on her hips and dug her heels into the gravel. "Have you been following me?"

"Didn't need to. I had a tip you were headed out here today." He grabbed her arm. "Let's sit down at that picnic table under the tree. The guards won't mind."

"H-how did you know? You know about my father, Eli Prescott, don't you?"

He brushed off a spot on the bench and waved her to sit. "I'm in the information business, beach girl."

"When did you find out?"

"After I left you yesterday. Could've bowled me over with a grain of sand."

Riley straddled the bench and Amy swung her legs over and leaned on the attached table. Riley still maintained his easy manner, but a new wariness had crept into his blue eyes. Heck, that always happened when people found out her identity, but she couldn't suppress the stab of disappointment that Riley followed suit.

He placed his hands on his knees, lifting his shoulders. "Why didn't you tell me your father was involved in dealing drugs?"

Amy's jaw dropped. He suspected her of…something, something more than just being the daughter of an imprisoned militia leader. "Wait a minute."

He quirked one brow, but his jaw hardened. "I have all the time in the world."

"Do you think I had something to do with Carlos's plans with the Velasquez Cartel?" The words spoken aloud sounded wild, crazy, but this stranger in the expensive getup didn't even crack a smile.

"You have to admit, it's a coincidence. Daughter of a former drug dealer involved with another drug dealer, dead bodies in her house, drugs on her beach."

"I wouldn't call my father a drug dealer."

"Defending him?"

"Never." She slammed her palms against the picnic table. "That's not what I meant. Dear old Dad was involved in all kinds of illegal activities. He used the militia front to make his endeavors sound more noble or worthy, but really he just led a cult and engaged in criminal behavior to get money to keep it going."

"And one of those illegal activities was dealing drugs." Riley rubbed a hand across his face and closed his eyes. "What do you expect me to think?"

"I don't expect you to think the worst of me. I gave you the benefit of the doubt when I stumbled across you on the beach after you'd just killed a man."

He clenched his eyes briefly before opening them. "I'll give you the benefit of the doubt if you start coming clean."

"I am clean." She spread her hands in front of her as the lie tumbled from her mouth.

"Why didn't you say anything about that cigarette holder we found in the storage unit with your father's initials inscribed on it? You recognized it immediately, didn't you?"

Amy pinched the bridge of her nose. "You're good."

"My contacts are good. Did you rush out here to San Miguel to find out if your father had snuck out to facilitate another drug deal and happened to drop his holder?"

She snorted. "Obviously not. I wanted to find out if anyone had those cigarette holders."

"Did he tell you?"

"He told me to leave it alone."

"Maybe he's looking out for your welfare."

Amy laughed, tipping her head back to the sky. "That would be a first."

"Someone needs to."

Her head snapped forward, and she huffed out a breath. "I think I'm capable of looking out for myself."

"In normal circumstances, but these aren't normal circumstances."

"My life has never consisted of normal circumstances. I'm accustomed to drama."

"I know." Riley brushed a lock of hair from her face, tucking it behind her ear. "Foster care must've been tough."

Amy squared her shoulders, her lips twisting into a halfhearted smile. "It was no picnic, but I got through it—with the help of my friend Sarah."

"Good, and now you're going to get through this with my help." He chucked her under the chin. "For the first time in your life, maybe you should listen to your father. Stay out of this."

"If he's telling me to butt out, it's for his own good,

not mine. I think I have a right to know who nominated me to be Carlos's cohort."

A crease formed between Riley's eyebrows. "So you *do* think your father is mixed up in this?"

"I'm not sure if he's involved directly, but he may know something."

"What makes you think that?"

"He told me not to get involved, didn't he? Why would he care otherwise?"

"Do you think he knows where the cigarette holder came from?"

Amy caught her breath and grabbed the material of Riley's dress shirt. "He said something about my siblings."

Riley reached into his shirt pocket and pulled out a folded piece of paper. He flattened it out on the picnic table, running his finger along the creases. "Is this your family?"

Amy peered at the picture printed in muddy colors from a laser printer. Her gaze scanned the women and children in the photo and tears pooled in her eyes as she pressed her locket against her chest. Those other women had been like second mothers to her, but the U.S. government had ripped her away from them.

One fat tear rolled over her lower lid and splashed on the page. "Th-that's my family. My father's other wives and their children. I was my mother's only child. Those are my half siblings."

"Are you in touch with any of them?" Riley blotted the circle of moisture with his thumb.

"No. Social Services took me away from the others because I had a different mother. When I was a child, I had no opportunity to reach them. When I became an adult, I had no desire."

Riley's finger traced along the back row of children in the picture, along the taller kids, the teens. "You must remember them."

She flicked at the faces with her finger. "Maisie got the hell out, Ethan was an SOB, Rosalinda married a Mexican national…"

"Ethan?" Riley swept the photo from the table and held it close to his face.

She wrinkled her nose. She hadn't thought about Ethan in years. "Ethan was the oldest and a bully. He idolized Dad."

"Did he smoke?"

"Smoke?" Her heart skipped a beat. Could it really be that easy?

Riley smacked the photo with his hand. "If he smokes and admired his father, he just might have a cigarette holder with his initials—*E.P.* Just like Dad."

Chapter Eight

Amy caught her bottom lip between her teeth, and her dark eyes widened. She choked out, "Do you think my half brother is working with Carlos?"

She had to be one heck of an actress if she was really involved in all this. Riley didn't give a damn about Eli Prescott or Ethan Prescott for that matter. A rush of warm relief had flooded his senses once he'd determined that Amy was as unaware and baffled by Carlos's nefarious connections as she appeared to be that first night on the beach.

As they peeled back every layer of the onion skin, Amy's danger from the Velasquez Cartel grew stronger. Had her own half brother set her up? Did they want something from her now?

"What do you know about your brother, Ethan?"

"I know I didn't like him. He bullied the rest of us and worshipped Dad. He almost wanted a confrontation with the Federales. I guess he hadn't counted on the Mexican government cooperating with the FBI."

Amy's father had to have been involved in some big-time crime for the Feds to step into a foreign country. "Where is he today?"

Amy shook her head, her long ponytail shimmering in the summer sun.

Riley folded the printed picture and ran his thumb along the crease. "Did Ethan ever try to contact you?"

"No. Not that he would've gotten very far. I didn't like him when I was a child. I can't imagine the raid on the compound and the circumstances of Dad's arrest would've turned him into someone I wanted to know."

"In fact, it could've turned him into a criminal."

"That wouldn't have been a huge leap for Ethan."

"Maybe Ethan was aware of your job and your location and set up the exchange thinking you'd help, given your history with law enforcement."

"I guess." Amy snatched the picture from the picnic table and smoothed it out. "I can't believe he tracked me down and actually thought I'd meekly agree to stash drugs on the beach."

Riley lifted a shoulder. "You guys had the same upbringing. You're not exactly a big fan of law enforcement, are you?"

"Distrusting the long arm of the law and engaging in criminal behavior are two different things."

"Not to Ethan." He pointed to the crinkled picture. "Do you want to keep that?"

"No, thanks." She shoved it back at him and swung her legs over the bench. "I'm going to get back to my friends' place."

"Maybe that's a good idea. Are you finished sleuthing around?" He hoped so. The more she dug into Carlos's motives, the more she exposed herself to danger.

"I just wanted to find out why Carlos used me, and what my father's cigarette holder was doing in the storage bin. I have answers to both of those questions. I'm done."

Riley expelled a breath and crumpled the picture of her family in his fist. He shoved it into his pants' pocket. *Out of sight, out of mind.* "Yeah, get back to your friends' place. That's the safest place for you. At this point, your involvement is over."

Nodding, she blinked rapidly. "I agree. I'm no threat to my brother or his business associates, and I'm certainly no threat to Carlos."

A muscle twitched in Riley's jaw. Was it all just wishful thinking? He couldn't shake the unanswered questions that threatened Amy's safety, but he couldn't shake the dread he felt keeping her with him. Those around him usually ended up burned—or worse.

"Is something wrong?" Her eyebrows shot up over a pair of wide eyes.

What happened to his poker face? Riley ran his palm across his smoothly shaven chin. "Why was Carlos at your place after the drop?"

She jerked her shoulders. "We've been through this a million times. Maybe he was on the run and went to the closest place he knew. The guys he ripped off followed him and killed him."

"Who'd he rip off—his own associates or their clients? I wonder if the men who killed him ever found what they were looking for."

"Well, I can't help them there." Amy brushed her hands together and placed them on her hips.

Did she want him to offer his protection? With his record, she'd be safer on her own. "I'll walk you to your car."

Her shoulders rolled forward before she stalked

toward the parking lot. Looked like she didn't even want this level of protection from him.

When she reached her car, she spun around and thrust out her hand. "Okay, well, good luck sorting this all out. If you run across my brother, tell him thanks a lot."

Definitely didn't want his protection.

He took her hand and clasped it between both of his. "I'm sorry I went digging around in your past. I just wanted to make sure—"

She twisted out of his grip. "You wanted to make sure I wasn't in cahoots with Carlos. I get it. I'm not the most trustworthy person in the world, and you figured that out pretty quickly."

"That's not true, Amy." He reached for her hand again and lightly twined his fingers with hers. "I knew you were hiding something about that cigarette holder. I never suspected your complicity before that, and I don't now."

"You don't have to explain anything, Riley. I know you want to help your friend. I understand that."

He brought her hand to his lips and kissed her damp palm. He wanted to do so much more, but her narrowed eyes and stiff spine screamed *back off.*

He reached around her and opened the car door. She slid inside, and he held the door. "You have my cell number. If anything happens, if you need any help, give me a call."

"I think you're the one who needs to be careful now." She snatched the door from his hand and slammed it.

Riley had no intention of allowing her to peel out of the prison parking lot without him. He could at least make sure no one followed her. He rushed to his car and beat her to the exit. Then he followed her down the highway.

His gut twisted when she put on her signal to take the next exit. He wanted to keep her with him and protect her.

Except the last woman who came to him for protection wound up dead.

Amy beeped her horn as she swerved onto the off-ramp and Riley flashed his lights. She might be done digging for answers, but he'd just begun. And he planned to start with Ethan Prescott.

When Riley arrived back at his house, he opened his laptop and got on the phone. He may be a dive-boat operator in Cabo, but he still had his law enforcement connections. He started with the San Diego Sheriff's Department and a former member of Riley's first SEAL unit, Walt Moreau.

"What would you spooks do without us regular cops?"

Riley snorted. "We'd be lost without you, but we spare you the ugly stuff."

"Yeah, right. You guys cause us more trouble than you're worth. I thought you were retired from spying, too."

"I did retire. I'm back for an encore. Long story."

"I don't wanna know. What do you need this time?"

"Ethan Prescott. Does he live here? Does he have a rap sheet? Is he a known drug dealer?"

Walt swore. "That SOB." He clicked some keys on his computer. "He's been in for a few petty crimes, but we can't nail him on the big stuff. He's a facilitator. Takes his cut for brokering deals."

"Do you have an address on him?"

"You paying him a social call?"

"Something like that. I'm real social when I want to be."

Walt gave him an address for Prescott in San Diego with his usual admonition. "You didn't get this from me."

Riley punched the address in on his GPS and followed the directions to Amy's brother's place in La Jolla, a well-heeled area of San Diego. The house was located near where Amy was staying. *Lifestyles of the rich and criminal.*

Riley pulled up across the street from a big, well-lit property. Cars lined the street in front of the house. Dinner party? That would work, and he still had on his slacks and dress shirt from the visit to the penitentiary. Hell, he was feeling social.

He marched up the walkway and pressed the doorbell. A member of the catering staff answered the door. First class all the way.

Riley pasted on his smoothest smile. "Good evening."

"Do you have an invitation, sir?" The party guests murmured behind him, clinking glasses. Sounded like a blast.

"Yes." Riley squared his shoulders and shook out his cuffs.

The man coughed. "Do you have it with you?"

Riley patted his pockets. "Looks like I forgot it."

"I'm sorry, sir. You have to have an invitation." The man's lips pursed as he folded his arms.

Riley rolled his eyes. Like this dude with his black apron and bow tie was going to keep him away from

Ethan Prescott. "I'm sure if you tell Mr. Prescott his sister's friend is here, he'll make an exception."

"His sister?"

"Amy."

The waiter held up his hand. "Wait here, please."

When he walked away, Riley stepped into the foyer and clicked the door behind him. The caterers had gone all out for this party. The smell of sizzling steak made his mouth water, and he closed his eyes as his stomach rumbled in protest. He could've at least bought Amy some dinner.

"You know Amy?"

The sharp words jerked Riley out of his food fantasies, and his eyelids flew open. The tall, angular man in front of him clutched a wineglass in one hand and a fork in the other.

Riley's gaze darted between the hovering caterer and Ethan Prescott's lean, hard face. "I do."

Prescott jerked his thumb at the waiter. "Get lost."

He turned back to Riley, his blue eyes glittering. "What do you want?"

"What do you want? Why are you following me? If you want to kill me for killing one of your guys, here I am." Riley spread his arms wide and grinned.

Prescott took a swig of wine and gestured to his left. A tall, beefy guy with a neck like a tree trunk emerged from the shadows. He shoved Riley against the wall and patted him down.

He grunted, "He's clean."

Riley had more sense than to bring a weapon—or wear a wire to a dinner party.

Prescott handed the fork to his henchman and adjusted his collar. "Who are you? CIA? Private investigator? I know you're not law enforcement. They're too polite to barge in unannounced like this."

"Yeah, I'm not polite at all." Riley smoothed his shirt. "I'm investigating another case and the Velazquez deal crossed into my radar, and then you crossed into my radar."

"I'm not following you, and that wasn't one of my guys. I'm just the broker. I don't give a rat's ass what happens to the two parties."

"Why did you involve your sister?"

Prescott swirled his wine. "You want a glass?"

"No." Riley shoved a clenched fist in his pocket. "Your sister?"

"I needed to find a drop location. That storage bin looked perfect, and I needed access. Pretty simple. I thought I could get her to work with me. I know she has no love for law enforcement, but Dad figured she wouldn't give me the time of day. So I used my charming friend, Carlos."

Riley scooped in a deep breath. Amy was just a means to an end. Nothing more. "What do you think happened to Carlos?"

"He disappeared."

"He's dead."

Prescott clicked his tongue. "This is a high-risk business. That's why I have bodyguards."

"If Carlos double-crossed someone, doesn't that put you at risk? He *was* your guy."

Prescott lifted one eyebrow. "Not really. Velasquez had used him before. I did my part. They can try to come after me, but Carlos is the one who took the clients' money."

Riley whistled. "Is that what happened? The Velasquez Cartel entrusted Carlos with the money to give to the terrorists in exchange for the drugs, and he stole it instead?"

Prescott whistled back. "You're good. I didn't even know the identity of the clients."

"Did the so-called clients get their money back when they murdered Carlos?"

A smile spread across Prescott's face, and Riley flinched at the pure evil emanating from the man. How could he and Amy be related? They didn't even seem like the same species.

"No, I don't believe they did get their money back."

"Is that why they're still on my tail? They think I have it or something?" Riley clenched his jaw. He'd have to disabuse them of that notion—fast.

Prescott chuckled and shook his head. "They're not after you. They're after Amy."

WHEN RILEY FLASHED HIS LIGHTS as Amy had careened onto the off ramp, she had to blink back tears to focus on the road. She knew Riley would've stayed with her if she'd begged, but she had too much pride for that. Her desire for his company didn't have anything to do with fear and everything to do with her attraction to him.

But he seemed determined to keep his distance. It was almost as if he considered himself toxic, but he was torn between that and his protective instincts which ran strong and deep.

She probably could've played on that aspect of Riley's character, but that was stooping pretty low. She didn't play games with men. Maybe that's why she didn't have one in her life.

Her stomach growled and she rubbed it. She should've

suggested dinner. He would've gone for that, figuring they could at least eat together without putting her life in danger.

Before making the turn to Sarah's house, Amy pulled into the parking lot of a shopping center with a bookstore, a coffee place, a bank and several restaurants. She stopped in at the bookstore first. Had to have something to read at dinner so she wouldn't look like a total loser eating by herself.

She tucked the glossy magazines under her arm as she pulled open the door to a small Japanese restaurant. She turned down the Saki in favor of a large ice tea and ordered some sushi and tempura. As if she didn't get enough fish.

When she finished her meal, she left one of the magazines on the table for the next loner to enjoy and stepped into the breezy evening.

Several turns and several miles later, she pulled into the long drive of Sarah's house and threw her car into Park. Closing her eyes, she leaned her head back and sighed.

The events of the day had drained her emotionally. She hadn't visited her father in a few years. He had nothing she wanted anymore. Still didn't.

She slipped into the house, flicked on the light and locked the door behind her. She kicked off her flats and padded across the cool tile of the kitchen floor. She needed more caffeine to stay awake and figure out the rest of her life. Grabbing a soda from the fridge, she cocked her head at a tinkling sound from upstairs.

She snapped the lid of her can and trudged up the curved staircase, straightening a picture on the wall on her way up. She paused on the landing while slurping

Get 2 Books FREE!

Harlequin® Books,
publisher of women's fiction,
presents

◆ **HARLEQUIN**®

INTRIGUE®

GET 2 BOOK

We'd like to send you two *Harlequin Intrigue*® novels absolutely free.
Accepting them puts you under no obligation to purchase any more books

HOW TO GET YOUR
2 FREE BOOKS AND 2 FREE GIFTS

1. Return the reply card today, and we'll send you two *Harlequin Intrigue* novels, absolutely free! We'll even pay the postage!

2. Accepting free books places you under no obligation to buy anything, ever. Whatever you decide, the free books and gifts are yours to keep, free!

3. We hope that after receiving your free books you'll want to remain a subscriber, but the choice is yours—to continue or cancel, any time at all!

EXTRA BONUS

You'll also get two free mystery gifts! (worth about $10)

FREE!

Return this card today to get
2 FREE BOOKS and 2 FREE GIFTS!

 HARLEQUIN®

INTRIGUE®

YES! Please send me 2 FREE *Harlequin Intrigue®*
novels, and 2 free mystery gifts as well. I understand
I am under no obligation to purchase anything, as
explained on the back of this insert.

*About how many NEW paperback fiction books have
you purchased in the past 3 months?*

❑ 0-2   ❑ 3-6   ❑ 7 or more
E9PD   E9PP   E9PZ

❑ I prefer the regular-print edition   ❑ I prefer the larger-print edition
182/382 HDL   199/399 HDL

FIRST NAME	LAST NAME

ADDRESS

APT.#	CITY

STATE/PROV.	ZIP/POSTAL CODE

Visit us at:
www.ReaderService.com

▼ DETACH AND MAIL CARD TODAY! ▶

(H-I-03/11)

If offer card is missing, write to: The Reader Service, P.O. Box 1867, Buffalo, NY 14240-1867 or visit www.ReaderService.com

BUSINESS REPLY MAIL

FIRST-CLASS MAIL   PERMIT NO. 717   BUFFALO, NY

POSTAGE WILL BE PAID BY ADDRESSEE

THE READER SERVICE
PO BOX 1867
BUFFALO NY 14240-9952

NO POSTAGE
NECESSARY
IF MAILED
IN THE
UNITED STATES

a sip of soda. The tinkle of the wind chimes floated through the door of the master bedroom. She poked her head around the corner, frowning at the curtains billowing into the room. A gust of wind sent the wind chimes into overdrive.

Sarah had mentioned her maid would be coming in today. Had she opened the window? The wind was kicking up from the ocean now strong enough to blow over those pretty little glass figures littering Sarah's dresser. Amy put her soda can on top of the dresser, and then paused to admire the view before sliding the window closed and clicking it into place.

She brushed some sand from the windowsill into her palm and dusted off her hands into the toilet in the master bathroom. A rustling noise from outside the bedroom caused her to freeze. A tingle raced up her spine.

The Lynches had boarded their dog before they left for vacation, but the girls had a hamster. It was probably Chester the hamster making all that racket. Please be Chester the hamster.

Amy tiptoed back into the master bedroom and peeked around the corner into the hallway, holding her breath. The rustling stopped. She'd better check on Chester in the kids' playroom.

She glanced into the guest bedroom and stumbled to a stop. Her suitcase, which she hadn't unpacked yet, gaped open on the bed. Its contents spilled over the sides and lay scattered across the floor.

Amy gripped the doorjamb for support, her gaze darting around the room. Someone had tossed the room—no other word for it.

The open window.

Her heart slammed against her rib cage and a cold chill ran through her body. Clenching her chattering teeth, she twisted to see over her shoulder. A shadow passed across the playroom door.

She had to get out of the house. Now.

Chapter Nine

Amy spun around and dashed for the stairs. As she reached the top step, she heard a footfall behind her. Clutching the banister, she took the steps two at a time, her feet barely skimming the tile.

When she reached the bottom and took the corner, her shoulder glanced off the wall. She gasped in pain. She scrambled for the front door, bracing her back for an attack and sucking in air to let loose with a scream when it happened.

She may not be ready with a weapon if someone grabbed her from behind, but she'd be ready with a scream loud enough to pierce his eardrums.

She shoved open the door and stumbled down the steps. She had no purse, no keys, no phone. The long driveway stretched in front of her, and she sprinted toward the street.

Tires squealed and a car blew up the drive. Amy dived to the side, landing in a clump of bushes. She screamed and thrashed until she tore herself away from the clinging twigs of the shrubbery.

"Amy!"

That voice. The small blue compact car. Help. Safety. *Riley.*

Sobbing, she stumbled toward him. He reached for her, and she threw herself against his chest. He held her. He soothed her. He didn't seem at all surprised.

"What happened, Amy?"

With her head still buried in his shoulder, she pointed toward the house. "There's someone in the house."

His frame hardened and coiled beneath her. "Right now?"

"I don't know. I think so. Someone searched my bag. I heard footsteps and took off."

With one arm curled around her waist, Riley ducked into his car and withdrew a gun. He started for the house, clinching her to his side. "I'm not leaving you. Not this time."

In her haste to flee the house, she'd left the door wide open. Brandishing his weapon, Riley crept into the foyer. "Did you actually see anyone?"

"N-no." Her gaze darted around the family room. "I saw an open window and my disheveled suitcase. Then I heard some noises and saw a shadow, which sent me flying down the staircase. I thought someone was coming after me."

Riley marched across the family room toward the dining room. He leveled a finger at the sliding door, open to the back patio and the beach beyond. "Did you leave that open?"

"No. He must've slipped out the back while I was running helter-skelter out the front."

"Or he was coming after you until he heard my car in the drive."

Amy folded her arms across her belly as a chill snaked up her spine. "Why?"

"We'll get to that." He smoothed his hands down her back. "Let's secure this door first and check upstairs."

She followed Riley up the staircase, and they visited each room, searching the closets and under the beds. Chester the hamster was spinning on his wheel, his little feet responding to all the excitement.

They ended up in Amy's room, her rifled suitcase a stark testament to the danger that stalked her.

She sank onto the bed, slouching forward. "What do they want from me, Riley?"

"They want their money."

She jerked her shoulders back. "What?"

"The men who delivered the drugs from Afghanistan want their money. They have big plans for that cash."

She sprang from the bed and grabbed his forearm. "Terrorists are after me?"

"They think you have their money. They believe that's what Carlos was doing at your house."

"Stashing money from a drug deal? But where? I'm assuming they're looking for a lot of cash. It would have to be in a bag or a suitcase." She flipped down the lid of her own bag. "And not one filled with women's clothing."

Riley shook his head and raked back his long hair from his forehead. "They think you have something. And they want it."

Amy paced toward the window and then spun around. "Wait a minute. How do you know all of this? Two hours ago at the penitentiary you were convincing both of us that the bad guys wanted you."

"Your brother told me."

She dropped to the bed again, like a boxer taking one to the gut. "You spoke to Ethan?"

"I met him." He settled next to her on the bed and draped his arm across her shoulder. "After I left you, I went on a mission to find your brother."

"Did he confirm that he set me up with Carlos?"

"He did."

Riley rubbed a circle on her back as if that could assuage the misery of your own half brother setting you up with criminals and terrorists. Amy closed her eyes and breathed deeply through her nose. The pressure of Riley's hand did help a little. Okay, it helped a lot.

"Ethan told you these men from some terrorist cell—" butterflies whirred in her belly at the words "—think I have their money?"

"That's the word on the street."

"My name is on the street?" She launched from the bed and away from Riley's comfort. Couldn't get too accustomed to his protection. "That can't be good."

"None of it's good, Amy. I don't want to scare you, but…" He grabbed a couple of fistfuls of bedspread and clenched his jaw.

"Don't stop now." She leaned against the wall, pressing her clammy palms against the smooth surface. She'd take whatever he had to throw at her standing up, not crouched on the floor like a quivering mass of jelly.

"Whoever searched this house didn't follow you here. I made sure of that."

She swallowed and squeezed her eyes shut briefly. "And that means…?"

"They know about you. They know your friends and your habits."

"But I don't have their money. Once they figure that out, they'll leave me alone."

"Don't you?" He pushed up from the bed and strode

toward her, sweeping his gun from the dresser on his way.

Amy's gaze shifted from the weapon in his hand to the dark blue eyes beneath disheveled hair. Was he back to that again? "You think I worked this out with Carlos?"

"No." He tucked the weapon in the back of his waistband. "Maybe you have the money and you just don't know you have the money."

"Uh, I'm pretty sure I'd know if I had—what?— several hundred thousand dollars on my person or in the trunk of my car."

"If Carlos had cash on him." Riley rubbed the dark gold stubble on his chin.

Amy dragged her gaze away from his sexy scruff and blinked. "What do you mean? You lost me."

"Carlos didn't stash a load of money at your house, but what if he left the means to get that money?"

She snorted. "Like a treasure map?"

Riley snapped his fingers in front of her face. "Think, Amy."

She ran her hands over her face and twirled her ponytail around her hand. She could think more clearly if she couldn't smell Riley's musky scent every time he touched her. And a lot more clearly if he didn't touch her at all.

Studying his blue eyes, all lit up with excitement, Amy nodded. "You mean like the number to a Swiss bank account or something?"

He clapped his hands. "That's the idea. He planned to steal that money. He coordinated the drug drop at the storage bin and then hightailed it to your place to claim his ticket for the money. Only the Velasquez Cartel was one step ahead of him. When the money didn't turn up at the conclusion of the deal, they came after him."

Amy marched to the bed and dug through her tousled clothing. "What could it be? Where could it be? I need to somehow convince the men after me that I don't have what they want."

"You must have it." He did a double take and then raised his brows. "You don't propose working with the terrorists to find their money, do you?"

"Of course not." Her cheeks heated. He still didn't completely trust her.

He shrugged his shoulders. "Then it doesn't matter what they think. They won't believe you anyway."

"When am I ever going to feel safe again?" She gripped her upper arms, allowing a rare bout of self-pity to wash over her in a wave so strong, her knees buckled.

Riley caught her in his arms, and she burrowed into his shoulder, ashamed of her pitiful weakness.

He whispered against her hair. "I'll protect you, Amy."

He sounded so sure and strong, she almost believed him. She straightened her spine jerking out of the embrace. "How? I can't help these people even if I wanted to." She held up her hands. "And I don't want to."

"You're coming with me." He squeezed her shoulder. "We'll figure this out together. Once that money is in the hands of the proper authorities, you'll be safe."

"I won't be safe until then?"

His mouth tightened and storm clouds rolled across his blue eyes. "Nothing's a sure thing."

She pushed away from him and began stuffing her

clothes back into the suitcase. "Well, that's a resounding endorsement of your capabilities."

"Just don't say I didn't warn you."

She spun around at the harshness of his tone. The pain etched across his face caused a lump to form in her throat. What happened to the easygoing surfer dude? "I—I'm sure I'll be better off with you than on my own."

He stuffed his hands into his black slacks and lifted his shoulders. "Let's lock up here and get back to my place. Maybe we should swing by your house first and do a thorough search. You didn't spend much time there after we found Carlos's body. You don't know what he might have left as a parting gift."

"You're sure my brother doesn't have any idea?"

"He didn't seem too concerned. He got paid up-front for facilitating the deal."

"He wouldn't be above turning on Carlos. Look what he did to me, and we're related."

"Stuff in the bathroom?" He jerked his thumb over his shoulder, and she nodded.

Amy left a note for Sarah and Cliff. Then they locked up the house and headed for the driveway, deciding to take both cars.

"What did you do with Carlos's car?"

"I dumped it. Not my style." He gestured to the little blue compact. "I'll follow you, and I'll look out for anyone following me."

"Funny how you're the secret agent and it was me they were after all along."

"Don't flatter yourself too much. I'm sure they'd be happy to see me out of the way."

"Guess we were just born under a couple of lucky stars, huh?"

He cocked his head. "I never considered myself very lucky…up until now."

He ducked into his car and slammed the door before she had a chance to ask him to clarify that. A warm thrill had coursed through her body at his words and the look in his eyes. If she had to choose anyone in the world to hide out with, it would be Riley Hammond.

She started her car and followed him down the driveway. He hadn't wanted her with him because he doubted his own ability to keep her safe, but why? He seemed to have supreme confidence in everything else he did.

It took nerves of steel to march up to her brother and demand answers. He could've been walking right into a nest of snakes. In fact, *snake* was an apt word for Ethan.

She flipped on her turn signal and watched in her rearview mirror as Riley's car followed her onto the highway. They had to find this money. What would a bunch of terrorists want with her after that?

What would Riley want with her after that?

Good news—find the money. Bad news—never see Riley again.

She let out a long breath. Just her luck to meet a hot new guy at the same time a terrorist cell was hot on her heels.

Who was she kidding? She'd lived with that kind of luck all her life. She gripped the steering wheel. *Get serious, Amy.* She searched her mind for anything Carlos might have said or done regarding money or bank accounts. She drew a blank. They never talked about stuff like that. He'd been too busy impressing her with his vast knowledge of art and literature, and she'd fallen for it like a ton of bricks.

Glancing in her mirror, she hit her signal for the off-ramp. The comforting glow of Riley's headlights shined into her back window. Her car crawled onto her dark street. She'd forgotten to leave a porch light on when she left and she had nothing on a timer.

She just hoped the neighbor girl was taking pity on Clarence.

She swung into her driveway and Riley pulled up to the curb. He landed on the sidewalk before she even opened her car door.

"Nobody followed us?"

"Would I be standing here calmly if they had?"

She wagged her finger at him. "No need to get testy."

"Is it dark enough out here?"

"I did leave in a hurry, remember? You're the one who hustled me out of here."

He dug the heels of his hands into his eyes. "I'm on edge."

"You and me both."

She stumbled over the porch step and Riley grabbed her waist from behind. His large hand rested on her hip and she gulped. The terrorists weren't the only ones keeping her on edge.

With a shaky hand, Amy inserted her key into the dead bolt. At least this time the dead bolt was locked. The unlocked dead bolt should've warned her last time. She eased open the door and flicked on the lamp nearest the entryway.

Her gaze tracked across the small living room and she took a step back to feel Riley's solid form behind her.

Yeah, these people were good.

Chapter Ten

Riley shifted to high alert as a little gasp escaped from Amy's lips and she fell against him. He tensed and wrapped one arm around her while reaching back for his weapon.

He whispered into her ear. "What is it?"

"They're back."

Riley tucked her behind him and crept into the room. At least this house was a lot easier to search than the Lynches' sprawling beach house. And he should know—this was his second go-around.

Amy clung to the back of his shirt as he moved through each room. He kept telling himself he didn't mind, but her growing dependence on him for protection filled him with cold dread. The circumstances of the past few days had thrust him into the role of protector, even though he'd vowed to forgo that particular pastime. Easier said than done—especially with a plucky woman in danger tripping over his feet at every turn.

Once he'd satisfied himself the house didn't contain any bogeymen, Riley collapsed on the couch. "You're sure they were here?"

Amy nodded. "Things are out of place, although I

don't have a clue why they're being so careful now after ransacking my suitcase at Sarah's house."

"They don't know that you're onto them. They could've searched this house yesterday." He checked the safety on his gun and placed it on the coffee table. "They obviously didn't find what they were looking for since they were at your friends' house today."

"I almost wish they'd just find their money and leave me alone." She folded her hands in her lap and slid a glance his way. "I know you think that's selfish, that I should be actively trying to keep the money out of their filthy hands."

He covered her clasped hands with one of his own. "I don't think that's selfish, Amy. I don't expect you to want to bring down a terrorist cell. That's completely out of your job description."

She turned her head, searching his face with an anxious look. "It's not because I'm on their side or I want to punish law enforcement, despite my crazy background and infamous family members."

"I know that, too." His gaze wandered around the room. "Of course, if we do find the money first and turn it over to the CIA, it will have the same effect. They'll leave you alone."

"I don't have any idea what Carlos could've hidden in my place or where."

Tilting his head back, he closed his eyes. "Let's think. He obviously didn't hide the money itself—too big, too noticeable."

"Did my brother indicate when the Velasquez people gave him the money to give to the clients?"

"In advance."

"So he had time to stash the money before the drop,

and he didn't hide it at my house. So where would you put that kind of cash for safekeeping? A bank?"

Riley opened one eye. "Never. It would leave a paper trail a mile long and Carlos wouldn't have wanted that. If he deposited it in an account, it would have to be some kind of offshore, untraceable one."

Amy sighed and hunched forward. "I just don't know. Why would Carlos leave anything with me? Did he hate me that much?"

Riley's fingers tingled to feel Amy's dark mahogany hair slip through his fingers as it slid across her back. He doubted Carlos hated Amy—probably felt damned lucky the Velazquez Cartel had chosen her as his dupe. Hiding his mode of access to the drug money with Amy had more to do with covering his own hide than endangering Amy. But that's exactly what Carlos had done.

Riley pushed up from the couch and extended his hand. "Let's get out of here. If the people who searched this house didn't find what they wanted, we won't either. Maybe they're wrong anyway."

She put her hand in his, and he pulled her up and toward him, so close he could see the gold flecks in her puzzled eyes.

He tried to reassure her. "Maybe Carlos headed back here after the drop because it was familiar territory. Maybe he never did leave anything in your possession."

Pressing her lips together, she shook her head. "That's even worse. As long as the terrorists think I have the money, it doesn't much matter whether I do or not. They're going to try to get it back."

Riley wrapped his arms around her, pulling her against his chest where he felt her heart galloping at a rapid pace. Then he said the dumbest thing he'd said in five years. "They'll have to come through me first."

BACK AT RILEY'S SAFE HOUSE Amy felt…safe, but it had nothing to do with the boxy, nondescript apartment and everything to do with the man at her side.

As Riley hauled her suitcase into the bedroom once again, Amy twisted the gold locket at her neck with nervous fingers.

"Do you always wear that necklace?" He walked into the kitchen and yanked on the fridge door.

She held the chain out with one finger and the large heart-shaped locket dangled from it. "It was the only thing I had left from my mother. That's why I wear it, even though it's too big and not stylish at all."

"Water?" He held up an empty glass. Amy nodded. "How'd your mother end up with a man like Eli Prescott?"

"The usual way, I guess. She fell in love with him."

"But he already had his harem going by the time she came to live with him, didn't he?"

"Yes." She dropped the locket where it thunked against her chest. "My father was a very persuasive man. We weren't the only family living at the compound. He'd convinced others to join us. He could convince anyone of just about anything."

"Too bad he used those talents in the wrong way." Riley handed her a glass of water.

She traced the rim of the glass with her fingertip. "The FBI charged onto that property and killed my mother."

Riley placed his hand on her lower back and guided her to the sofa. "I'm sorry, Amy."

"It should've been him." She gulped the water and slammed the glass on the coffee table. "They wanted him."

"And now your family has dragged you back into the muck with them." He massaged between her shoulder blades, and she leaned her elbows on her knees.

"I tried to make peace with my feelings for my father, but in the end decided to put it all behind me. I guess you can only run so fast before the bad stuff catches up to you."

"You don't deserve this, any of it."

The pressure of his hands grew harder, and she leaned into his strength, closing her eyes. She usually deflected others' sympathy and pity, but now she allowed herself to wallow in it. She'd been wallowing a lot these past few days—even crying. She hadn't permitted herself many tears over the years—too dangerous to show weakness.

He squeezed the back of her neck with one hand. "Did you get something to eat tonight?"

"Yeah, did you?" She rolled her head back, not wanting Riley's magic hands to stop.

"No. Your brother was having a swanky dinner party, but I had other plans."

She twisted around, cupping her chin in her palm. "Thanks again for coming to the rescue. You have a knack for that sort of thing, don't you?"

"As a Navy SEAL it's second nature, but..." He stopped and shrugged.

"I know. You're a dive-boat operator from Cabo now."

"And what about you, Amy?" He stroked her hair and she almost purred like her abandoned cat, Clarence.

"What do you do when you're not rescuing people from the ocean?"

"Well, before you killed a guy on my beach, I was planning to start EMT school in a few weeks and try to get on with a fire department in the next year or two."

He lifted one eyebrow. "Talk about being born to rescue. Why do you gravitate toward those professions?"

"I never thought of it as a gravitational pull." She avoided his piercing blue gaze. "I can pretty much do what I like anyway. I'm independently wealthy."

He started to snort and then ended on a choke. "You're serious, aren't you?"

"The FBI killed my mother. I got a fat settlement for that, which didn't start paying out until I was eighteen. My friend's husband, Cliff, is my attorney, and he's managed my money very well."

Riley whistled. "Maybe Carlos was after your money, too."

"I doubt it. He didn't know anything about my money."

"Played it kind of close to the vest with Carlos, didn't you?"

"We dated only a few months. I'm not going to spill my guts after two months of dinners and movies."

"You told me after two days of car chases and break-ins."

"That's different."

He cocked his head. "How so?"

Amy twirled a lock of hair around her finger. If she had to explain the connection she felt with him, the electricity that zapped her senses every time he touched her, then maybe her attraction was all one-sided. Maybe she'd better quit while she was ahead and not make a fool out of herself.

"Uh, you know. The excitement and adrenaline rush gives everything an urgency."

"Like this?" He pulled her into the crook of his arm, tilted her head back and kissed her mouth.

Guess he felt it, too.

Her mouth tingled as his gentle caress grew more demanding. A pulse throbbed in her bottom lip and she reached up and twined her fingers around his hair.

He shifted, pulling her across his lap and linking his hands behind her back. "I've wanted you in my arms like this for a long time."

She murmured against his mouth, "You've known me for less than three days."

"Must be that urgency thing you were talking about." He pinched her chin and ran his thumb across her mouth.

"Speaking of urgency—" she sat up "—I thought we were coming back to your safe house to figure out why these guys think I have the money from the drug deal gone bad."

"First things first. I brought you back to my safe house to keep you safe."

The way her brain fogged over every time Riley kissed her felt anything but safe, but it did feel…right.

"I'm glad we're putting off thinking about our problems, because I can't think straight when you're kissing me like…that." She sighed as his lips trailed across her throat.

"How about if I kiss you like this."

He planted a line of kisses along her jaw and ended with a kiss at the corner of her mouth. She couldn't figure out how such a hard man could have such soft lips. Then she was done figuring when he slipped his tongue between her lips and tickled the roof of her mouth.

A gasp escaped from her throat, half laugh, half moan. She dug her nails into his shoulders, searching for something steady to hold on to as he deepened his kiss and slid his hands beneath her T-shirt. His palms, calloused and rough, brushed her skin and she squirmed beneath his touch.

"Is this doing anything to help you think straight?"

She nipped his ear. "You know it's not. I don't get how you can engage in…a flirtation…when terrorists are hunting you down."

Technically, they were hunting her down, but Riley had taken her cause on as his own. And that was even sexier than his hands rubbing those little circles on her back. Almost.

His brows shot up to the shaggy hair falling across his forehead. "You call this a flirtation? I must be slipping."

He curled his hands around her waist, pulling her against his chest. Then he dipped his head and possessed her lips as if he didn't have one thought in his brain except pleasure. Her pleasure.

Without losing their connection, Amy fumbled with the buttons of Riley's shirt until it hung open on his chest. Then she yanked at the white T-shirt tucked into his slacks, scraping his flat belly with her fingernails. "You are way overdressed."

His gaze swept over her skirt and top, lingering on her bare legs hanging over his lap. "So are you."

He staggered from the couch, clutching her to his

chest. "Are we going to fumble around on the couch like a couple of teenagers?"

Shaking her head, she entwined her arms around his neck. "Take me anywhere, sailor."

In a few quick strides he shoved open his bedroom door with his shoulder and kissed her again before dropping her on the bed. Without losing eye contact, they both scrambled out of their clothes. Only then did Amy allow herself to savor Riley's naked body.

He had the perfect swimmer's form with his wide shoulders, broad chest, narrow hips and flaring thighs. Amy's lashes fluttered as desire coursed through her veins. Riley was no accountant or banker or plumber— probably didn't have one stable, boring bone in his body. But God she wanted him.

"Done with the inventory?" He grinned, his blue eyes shooting sparks.

She shrugged and faked a yawn. "Nothing I haven't seen a million times before."

Riley scrambled onto the bed and hitched her around the waist with one arm, dragging her against his hard planes. "How about I rock your world with something you haven't felt a million times before?"

Before she could answer in the affirmative, he landed a hard kiss on her mouth—punishment for her sarcastic tongue. Then he laid her out on the bed and used his tongue, which wasn't sarcastic at all, to bring her to dizzying heights of ecstasy.

Digging her nails into his muscled buttocks, she panted against his shoulder. "You made your point, sailor. Now finish the job."

"Don't forget." He cupped her breast in his hand and

massaged her nipple with his thumb. "I live in Mexico now. We take things slow and easy down there."

She squirmed from beneath the weight of his body and rolled on top of him. "I'll give you slow and easy."

She kissed his eyelids and the bridge of his prominent nose. Although the heat of her passion thumped with urgency, she closed her eyes and pressed her lips against the stubble along his jaw and twirled her tongue in the hollow of his throat.

He hissed and grabbed her hips, grinding his erection into her belly.

She nipped his earlobe. "Slow and easy, remember?"

He growled. "We're in *Los Estados Unidos* now, baby."

He flipped her onto her back and drove into her with such force she bumped her head on the headboard—and she didn't mind one bit. She thrust back against him, enjoying the ride, enjoying the thrill of having this dangerous, exciting man in her bed and in her life. She'd deal with the consequences later.

Like they'd known each other all their lives, they reached their climaxes together in perfect sync, noisily, heartily and completely. A matched pair.

Riley rolled to her side, but pulled her close to maintain their connection. He brushed a strand of hair from her lips, which parted with each short gasp of breath she took. "Too much for you?"

Narrowing her eyes, she slapped his backside with her palm. "I'm ready for another round."

He kissed the tip of her nose. "You're fearless in every situation, Amy, not like—"

Riley's cell phone rang from the pocket of his slacks, crumpled on the bedroom floor. He blew her a noisy kiss. "Keep the bed warm."

He launched off the bed and clawed through his pants to find the phone. "Hello?" His head shot up as three sharp knocks cracked on the front door.

A tingle of fear raced across Amy's flesh, chasing away desire. "Who is it?"

Riley tossed aside the phone and pulled on his slacks. "One of my brothers in arms."

Amy had dragged the sheet up to her chin and her long, dark hair tumbled around her face with its wide, glossy brown eyes and trembling lips, plump from his kisses. His need for this woman, still unabated, coiled hot and firm in his belly.

But duty called.

Ian Dempsey stood outside his front door, and he might have news of Jack.

Riley pulled his T-shirt over his head and pointed to the phone. "That was my buddy on the phone letting me know he's outside. Unfortunately, I have to let him in."

The strain on Amy's face smoothed out and she sighed. "Oh, of course. I'll get dressed."

"That's a good idea because that dude out there is a wolf." He winked and snapped the bedroom door behind him.

Riley shoved his eye against the peephole and scanned the tall man parked at his doorway. At least he'd called first instead of showing up unannounced—just might have saved himself from a bullet between the eyes.

Riley yanked open the door. "You do know this

is a safe house, don't you? You sure you weren't followed?"

Ian laughed and pushed his way into the apartment. "Good to see you, too, Riley. Besides we always had you pegged as the careless one."

Riley slammed the door and locked it. Then he thrust out his hand. "How the hell are you, man?"

Ian shrugged. "I've been better. They're calling Jack a traitor."

"I know." Riley balled his fists. "It's a lie."

"You don't have to convince me." Ian held up his hands. "This is a big-time operation. You don't think our old friends have anything to do with it, do you?"

"Why would they be out here now? They used to be strictly local." A bitter bile rose from Riley's gut when he thought about the team of terrorists operating in the Middle East that Prospero had repeatedly come up against. Prospero had almost taken down their leader, Farouk, on their last mission together.

"Those drugs came from Farouk's territory." Ian shrugged. "Whoever they are, they sold a lot of heroin to the Velasquez Cartel for a lot of money, and I don't think they plan to use the money to open flower shops."

"They've been linked to an arms dealer here in the States. We just need a name." Ian paced the room, absently picked up Riley's jacket, then dropped it.

"How is that going to get us closer to Jack?"

Ian spread his hands. "It's the whole setup. The entire deal is linked to some doctor who was kidnapped in Afghanistan. Jack was hired to negotiate for his release, and he disappeared."

"You know more than I do then. Do we have a name on the doc?"

"No name. It's hush-hush. We know his sister hired Jack, but we can't track her down."

"Did the colonel tell you I ran into a hitch here?" Riley ran his hands through his tangled hair; they had recently wound around Amy's fingers as he coaxed her to her climax. He swallowed.

"You tried to disrupt the deal, and now either the Velasquez Cartel or the client is after you."

"Actually, they're after me."

Amy strode into the room, looking a helluva lot more put together than he did in his dress slacks, un-tucked T-shirt and bare feet.

Ian's brows shot up and his gaze darted between Amy and Riley. "And you are?"

Riley stepped between them as if to shield Amy from Ian's scrutiny. "This is Amy Prescott, the lifeguard from the beach. Amy, this is Ian Dempsey, another former member of Prospero. He was in the Army Mountain Division and leads climbing expeditions now."

Amy maneuvered around him and thrust her hand out toward Ian. "Nice to meet you."

As he clasped her hand, Ian slid a glance toward Riley. "Good to meet you, too, but Colonel Scripps gave me the distinct impression the lifeguard was male."

Riley cocked his head. "Can't imagine why."

"I can." Ian gave Riley a hard stare.

Riley turned his back on Ian's accusing green eyes. "Do you want something to drink while we fill you in?"

"Soda or juice, whatever you have. I'll skip the beer."

Riley returned from the kitchen with a can of soda and thrust it into Ian's hand. "Have a seat."

Ian popped the lid and then aimed a finger, glistening with drops of soda, at Riley's hair hanging to his shoulders. "You look like the scruffy owner of a dive boat."

Riley pointed to Ian's dark hair—close-cropped and creating a cap around his head. "And you look like you never left the military."

Ian ran a hand over his short hair. "Habit."

Amy had gotten herself a glass of water and scrunched into the corner of the sofa, curling her long legs beneath her. "Are we going to tell him everything?" Riley asked her.

He studied Amy's face. He'd leave it up to her whether or not she wanted to reveal her personal connection to the events of the past few days. It was her life. Everyone had a right to a few secrets.

Her dark lashes swept her cheeks and she gave a brief nod.

"If we're going to help Jack, I think I need to hear everything." Ian perched on the stool at the kitchen counter, wrapping his hands around his soda.

Riley settled on the other end of the couch from Amy and drew a deep breath. He'd tell Ian everything from the beginning, everything except for his feelings for Amy, the way she made his head spin, the way her silky skin felt against his body, his intense desire to protect her. He'd keep all that to himself.

For the next hour, Riley told Ian about his tussle on the beach and the car chase and the discovery of Amy's identity and the realization that members of the terrorist cell were after Amy because they thought she had their money.

Ian asked the hard questions nobody could answer

and seemed to dodge around the relationship between Riley and Amy, accepting that Riley could keep Amy safe in his apartment while they worked through the puzzle of where Carlos hid the money.

Ian had drained his soda long ago and sat fiddling with the silver tab. "There is one option you haven't explored yet."

"I'm sure there are plenty of those." Riley pushed up from the couch and stretched. "More water, Amy?"

"No, thanks."

Riley swept up his own glass and ambled toward the kitchen. "What option are you talking about, Ian?"

Ian had worked the tab loose and dropped it into the can. "We want the name of their arms dealer and they want their money."

"So?" Riley dropped his glass in the sink harder than he intended and a crack zipped up the side.

Ian looked up from playing with his soda can and hardened his jaw. Riley knew that look. He didn't like it.

"Maybe we can offer an exchange."

"What?" Riley dropped the glass in the trash where it smashed against an empty jar. "We don't have anything to exchange, Ian. Weren't you listening? Amy doesn't have the money."

"The clients don't know that."

Riley laughed through gritted teeth. "Yeah, right. They'll find out soon enough. They're not going to give up the name of their arms dealer anyway. It would defeat the purpose of the whole operation. Dude, you've been spending too much time at high altitudes. It's turning your brain to mush."

Ian stood up and crushed the soda can. "It's just a

start, Riley. If your enemies think you have something they want, it can be a bargaining chip. You know that, or at least you used to. Maybe all that sun and surf are turning *your* brain to mush."

"I see what he means." Amy uncurled her legs and rose from the couch. "If they think I have their money, they might be willing to give you some information to get it back."

Riley's jaw dropped. "You two seem to be forgetting one important fact. We don't have their money."

"Think outside the box for a minute, Riley. You used to be so good at that." Ian slid a glance toward Amy.

Riley clenched his hands and stalked back into the living room. "Are you questioning my handling of this operation or my commitment to finding Jack?"

"Just wondering why you haven't come up with any options other than hiding in your safe house."

His blood boiling, Riley took another step toward Ian.

"Okay, you know what?" Amy stepped between them. "I'm really tired right now and I have a headache. I'm in no mood to watch a couple of grown men duke it out."

Riley let out a long breath. "Nobody's going to duke it out. We just have a difference of opinion. I have some ibuprofen in the bathroom."

When Amy left the room and closed the door of the bathroom, Riley turned on Ian. "I haven't been hiding in the safe house. I had to kill one of Velasquez's men when he threatened Amy on the beach. I had to track down her slimy half brother to gauge his involvement. I had to rescue her when some scumbag tracked her down to her friends' house and searched the place."

Ian grunted. "Yeah, I'm seeing a common theme here.

Are you interested in getting information about this deal or in protecting Amy?"

Riley dug his bare feet into the carpet to keep from launching across the few feet separating him from Ian and grabbing his throat. "Both. I'm doing both."

"Because it sounds to me like you're letting your feelings for Amy get in the way of your mission."

"You'd never do that, would you, Ian?" Riley crossed his arms over his chest. "That's why Meg left you. You'd never let your wife come before your duty."

Ian squared his shoulders, his green eyes glittering like chunks of glass. "Meg understood."

"Yeah, she understood. But she probably didn't understand completely until she lost the baby and you turned away from her."

"Damn you. I was on assignment."

"I understand, but she still left you."

Ian had lost his cool, a rare event. He slammed his fist on the counter, his voice exploding. "You're talking to me about *my* wife? What about your wife?"

"You have a wife?" Amy had left the bathroom and was leaning against the wall, her arms wrapped around her stomach.

And the look in her eyes twisted a knife in Riley's gut.

Chapter Eleven

Amy drove her shoulder into the wall, seeking support. Did her past make her some kind of magnet for married men looking for an escape? Oh right, she didn't know if Carlos really had a wife. He may have been a completely single drug dealer.

She hadn't meant to eavesdrop on Riley's conversation with Ian, but when their voices crescendoed in anger she'd worried about the two men coming to blows. Now the big, strong men, full of fury, looked like guilty little boys.

All the bluster had seeped out of Ian. He dropped his gaze from hers, running a hand across his short, dark hair.

Her eyes flicked to Riley. He seemed to have forgotten Ian's existence. A thousand different emotions charged across his handsome face until it settled into lines of concern.

At least she didn't discern any pity. She didn't like pity—from anyone.

She shoved off the wall and straightened her spine. "What were you saying about Riley's wife, Ian?"

Ian hunched his shoulders and rolled them back as if loosening the last grip of his anger. "I'm sorry, Riley.

I never should've thrown April in your face like that. Amy, it's not what it looks like. I'm sure Riley will explain everything."

Amy smirked because that seemed to stop the trembling of her lips. "Yeah, like how he gets it on with damsels in distress while his wifey is safely at home?"

Ian spread his hands in front of him, a helpless gesture from an anything-but-helpless man. In fact, Amy had a hard time believing these two men, with their athletic bodies and take-charge attitudes, couldn't bring down the terrorists and the Velasquez drug cartel by themselves. That Jack Coburn was one lucky SOB to have these two on his side.

"Tell her, Riley."

Riley seemed to wake up from his trance. He shook his head and rubbed his chin with its golden stubble. Reaching over, he clapped Ian on the shoulder. "I'm sorry, man. I know Meg never blamed you for the end of the marriage."

Amy folded her hands behind her back. She didn't want to hear about Ian's marriage, but at least the former colleagues weren't at each other's throats any more. She cleared her own throat.

"She didn't, but I did. You had it dead right." Ian shrugged off Riley's hand and walked toward Amy. "I know you're doing your best to help Jack, but you don't have anything to prove. What happened to April wasn't your fault, but you owe Amy the truth. Give her a chance to help you, Riley. She's not April."

Amy's mouth went dry, and she dropped her chin to her chest. What had happened to Riley's wife?

Ian took her hand. "You're an amazing woman, Amy. Riley's met his match."

Riley scooped in a big breath. "I will tell her as soon as you give us a little privacy. I've spilled my guts in front of you enough already. And you'd better savor that apology because it'll be another millennium before you hear another one out of me."

"I know that." Ian squeezed Amy's hand. He whispered, "Give him a chance to explain, Amy. Give him a chance."

When Ian shut the front door behind him, Riley stood with his back to her. His shoulders heaved before he turned around.

"I'm sorry." He smacked his forehead with the heel of his hand. "That's twice in one night."

Despite his easy words, Riley crossed his arms, digging his fingers into his bunched biceps.

Amy clutched her hands in front of her just as hard. "What happened to April?"

"I killed her."

Tilting her head, Amy raised one eyebrow. She didn't realize Riley had the capacity for so much melodrama. He had a lethal side, but she knew he'd never hurt a woman. Her next words almost stalled in her throat. "She's dead?"

He nodded. "April was my wife and she's dead."

Amy uprooted her feet from the carpet and almost tiptoed to Riley's side. Now she felt like a fool, a monster really for being jealous of a dead woman.

"How'd it happen?" She caressed his forearm—as hard as steel to match the blue steel of his eyes.

He blinked, the knuckles on his hand turning white and the veins popping on his corded arm. "She came to me for protection and I failed her."

Grabbing his hand, she pulled him away from the

door and led him to the couch. She leveled her palms on his chest and pressed firmly. "Sit."

He sank to the couch, his knees bumping the coffee table. "I didn't want to tell you about April. I wanted to keep you safe, not scare you away."

"You have kept me safe. I would've been toast without you." She rubbed a circle on his back, her hand skimming across hard slabs of muscle and tension. "Tell me what happened to April."

Riley dug the heels of his hands into his eyes and let out a shuddering breath. "April was from a wealthy family, the daughter of a politician. She'd had an easy life filled with easy opportunities and luxuries. She worked as a reporter and went along with her father to Iraq on a junket. That's where we met."

"You saw her in that dangerous setting and you wanted to protect her forever."

"I'm that transparent, huh?" He turned his head, plowing fingers through his hair.

Brushing the hair from his forehead, she whispered, "That honorable."

"I figured out quickly we'd made a mistake. She not only feared the atmosphere in Iraq but everywhere else—Italy, where we went on our honeymoon, and even San Francisco, where we'd settled between my assignments."

"She'd become accustomed to being well-guarded all her life?"

"Something like that—secret service, boarding schools, the works. When I'd leave her for missions, she'd call constantly, distracting me, making me feel guilty and miserable. She saw me not so much as a husband, but her own personal bodyguard."

"I know the feeling." She rubbed her hand along his thigh. "You do inspire that kind of confidence in a girl."

"It didn't quite work out that way. April imagined carjackers on every corner and peeping toms at every window. She didn't want to stay alone anymore and became convinced that she'd be safe only with me... even if that meant in Iraq."

Amy widened her eyes and covered her mouth with her hand. "She went back to Iraq?"

"Yes. And it was even less safe than before. She wasn't part of a large delegation of U.S. politicians this time."

"D-did you invite her to come out?"

"No." Riley smacked his palms on the coffee table. "She surprised me, used her connections to come out and faked an assignment. I was too busy at the time to send her right back home. I left her at what I thought was a safe hotel, but I should've known. Nothing is safe in Iraq."

"She felt safe with you, wherever that led her." She covered one of his large, rough hands with her own. "I can understand that."

"It's the opposite." Riley raked a hand through his hair. "Terrorists drove a car bomb into that hotel and fifteen people died, including April."

Amy sucked in a breath. April had been irrational following Riley to Iraq. Did she really believe she'd be safer in some hotel in Iraq than her upper-middle-class neighborhood in San Francisco?

She studied Riley's hard profile. She could understand April's compulsion to follow this man to the ends of the earth. April may have told Riley she felt safer with him, but maybe she just couldn't let her husband out of her sight.

Amy wouldn't be able to, if he belonged to her.

With a tight throat, she murmured, "It's not your fault, Riley. You didn't ask her to join you."

"But she did, and I didn't act quickly enough to send her back. Her closeness to me killed her. I'm a walking, living, breathing disaster area. Look at you."

"What?" She jerked her head, and her hair swept across their clasped hands. "I am not in danger because of you."

He slipped his hand from hers and massaged his temple. "I can't help thinking I'm bringing this all down on you. If I'd never landed on your beach, you'd be packing up for EMT school right now."

"That's just dumb. You didn't land on my beach. You followed a drug dealer to my beach, which had been chosen specifically because I worked there. My own crazy background catapulted me into this mess, and if you hadn't come along when you did, I'd be dead." She cupped his lean jaw with one hand. "So stop blaming yourself for my situation and maybe you'll eventually stop blaming yourself for your wife's death."

He closed his eyes. "April wasn't the only one who died. She was pregnant."

Amy's nose stung with tears as she trailed her thumb across Riley's lips. "I'm sorry."

Riley continued in a low voice, his eyes still closed. "I accused Ian of putting his job before his wife, but I did the same. April and I had discussed having kids, but I told her I wasn't ready. In fact, I'd started doubting the relationship would last much longer. She got pregnant anyway, but I never had to get used to the idea of becoming a father. I didn't have the chance."

He carried the guilt of his wife's death along with that of his unborn baby, as if his doubts about the marriage and his unwillingness to have children had contributed to the tragedy.

"Riley." She ran the pad of her thumb along his cheekbone. "Let go of the guilt."

His eyelids flew open and he grabbed her hands. "I'm not putting my job ahead of you, Amy. I'm not using you as some kind of bargaining chip with a bunch of thugs. Ian and his options can go to hell."

"We'll find the money. Once we do, maybe we can make our own deal with the arms merchant, a deal that could lead to information about Jack. We'll start fresh tomorrow."

Riley groaned. "God, what time is it? After everything you've endured today, I'm keeping you awake with my self-pitying story."

"There you go again." She kissed his rough cheek. "You don't need to look after me twenty-four hours a day. I can stand on my own two feet. I wouldn't be here right now if I couldn't."

He cupped the back of her head, entwining his fingers in her hair. "You're nothing like April, Amy, and God help me, I feel guilty about that, too."

"April made her choices. We all do." She tugged at his hand. "Let's get some sleep so we can brainstorm tomorrow. I think if Carlos did leave the money with me, he left it at my rental house. That makes the most sense since he returned there after dropping the drugs at the beach. Otherwise, why come back to my place?"

Riley followed her to the bedroom, resting a hand

on her hip. "That occurred to me, but someone made a thorough search of your place and came up empty. They wouldn't have tracked you down to the beach house if they'd found anything."

"Who knows if they searched the house completely? They don't even know what they're looking for."

"Neither do we."

Amy spun around and put two fingers to his lips. "Don't be so sure about that."

Riley captured her hand and placed a kiss on the center of her palm, his eyes alight with desire. She didn't know what Riley wanted, but she may have already found what she was looking for in the arms of this protective man.

Could she hold on to him when the danger dissipated? Would she want to?

THE FOLLOWING MORNING, Amy sat cross-legged on the floor of Riley's small apartment, balancing a notebook on her knees and tapping the end of her nose with a pencil. "We searched the entire house for a big bag of money, right? If Carlos didn't leave the money itself, he must've left a means to access it."

Riley hunched over his coffee, peering into the steaming, dark liquid. Coming clean about April had scattered the fog that had swirled around his relationship with Amy from the beginning, but he hadn't minded the murkiness.

He'd rather be tarred and feathered than peel back his armor to reveal his weaknesses and fears to anyone, especially a woman he'd vowed to protect. But Ian had forced him into it with his surprise visit. Riley didn't know what he'd expected after his confession, but it hadn't made Amy distrust him with her safety.

Opening up hadn't lessened his guilt any either. He'd carry that with him always.

"Don't you think?"

"Huh?" Riley glanced up from his mug.

Jabbing the air with her pencil, Amy said, "Access to the money. Where did Carlos leave the money and what did he leave in my house that would give him access to it? That's where I'm going with all this."

Riley sipped the strong brew and nodded. "I think you're right. Carlos wasn't going to haul around bags of cash with him. He stashed it."

"Do you think my brother could've been in on it? Maybe he and Carlos decided to double-cross the clients together, and then Ethan double-double-crossed Carlos." She swirled the pencil with a flourish.

Riley raised one eyebrow. When Amy attacked something, she went all out. He'd have to remember that. "That could be a possibility, but Carlos came back to your place not your brother's."

"You have a point, but I gather you didn't question Ethan very closely."

"Uh, no. Once he told me the terrorist cell had its sights set on you, I left the party."

"I'm glad you did." One corner of her mouth tilted up and Riley had a strong inclination to kiss it where it dimpled. She continued, oblivious to his desires. "But maybe we should pay another visit to Ethan to find out what he knows."

Riley choked and sprayed the countertop with coffee. "You want to see your half brother after all these years?"

"I think the situation warrants an impromptu family reunion. I visited my father in the Federal pen. What's one more disgraced family member?"

"I don't know, Amy." Riley grabbed a paper towel and blotted the drops of coffee. "You go to your family looking for answers and they turn against you. Why should Ethan tell you anything?"

"Couldn't you threaten him with something? Tell him you'll bring the FBI down on his head if he doesn't cooperate with us." She jabbed her chest with her thumb. "Ethan loves the FBI as much as I do."

Riley swept the soggy paper towel from the counter and tossed it into the trash. "I don't have anything on Ethan. I didn't have a recording device on me when he confessed to working with Carlos and the Velasquez Cartel. And, believe me, the FBI already has your brother on its radar, and he knows it."

Amy uncurled her long limbs and jumped to her feet. "Then I'll just use the old blood-is-thicker-than-water plan. What does he have to lose by telling me what he knows?"

"His life."

Amy's big eyes got bigger. "Do you think so?"

"If Velasquez's client believed your brother knew the location of that money, he'd be a dead man. Ethan wants to keep as far away as possible from you in case someone is watching him. He warned me not to return and definitely not to return with you in tow."

"Then we need to find a way to get to Ethan. You don't happen to have his cell phone number, do you?" Amy dug her teeth into her lower lip.

"No, we didn't make it to the let's-be-friends-and-exchange-numbers stage. But if you're serious, I can pay him a visit without anyone the wiser."

"*You* can pay him a visit? No, no, no." She waved her hands, the line of her jaw hardening.

Riley had hoped she hadn't noticed his use of the singular pronoun, but Amy had her own agenda now. And she was hell-bent on putting it into action. "It's safer if I go alone."

She cut him off, slicing her hand through the air. "I don't believe I'm safer away from you than with you, Riley. You're not some walking jinx. And I'm not April."

He flinched. The woman played hardball, but her stripping away of his private thoughts felt like a bracing blast of fresh, clean air. He filled his lungs.

"So let's pay Ethan that visit." She tossed her head, her dark hair whipping over her shoulder and her gold locket winking in the morning sun.

Riley nodded and held out his arms. She came to him, wordlessly and without hesitation. They held on to each other like a drowning couple clutching their last lifeline.

Then he kissed her temple and stared out the window over her head.

Riley Hammond, you just met your match.

AMY HUNCHED FORWARD, the black knit cap scratchy against her cheek. She tucked a finger inside the edge and ran it along the curve of her face. Riley hadn't been kidding about paying a covert visit to her half brother.

She twisted her head toward the dark street and swallowed. Did he really think some terrorist might be watching Ethan?

The white columns of Ethan's house gleamed in the moonlight, and a few windows from the upper story glowed with a faint yellow light. They'd been lucky Ethan hadn't been in full-entertainment mode tonight. They still didn't know whether or not he was home, but if not, they'd wait for him.

She'd wait a long time to get answers from her half brother.

Riley whispered, his words tickling her ear. "The street looks clear from here. When I ran a perimeter around the house, I spotted the box for the security system. Wait here while I disable it."

She twisted her hands together as Riley crouched and traveled swiftly across the lawn, barely disturbing a blade of grass.

She didn't want to stay ensconced in the bushes ringing Ethan's palatial house, every rustling leaf, every chirp from a cricket making the hair on the back of her neck quiver with fear. But hadn't she disassociated herself from April earlier?

Clamping her chattering teeth, she felt a strong kinship with Riley's fearful wife. Bravado caused you to do stupid things. She wasn't even sure if her plan was an effort to confront Ethan or just a ruse to gain Riley's admiration and undying respect.

She'd focus on undying for now.

A twig snapped beside her and she almost jumped out of her skin until Riley's face hovered in front of her. The man moved as stealthily as a panther. She hadn't even tracked his return to the foliage.

"Shh." He held up one hand. "It's done. We're going around to that back door I pointed out to you earlier."

Riley hadn't known if Ethan lived alone, had a wife

or children or had twenty-four-hour bodyguard protection. Guess they'd find out soon enough.

Doubling over, Riley emerged from the bushes again, and this time Amy followed him. He hadn't trusted her with a weapon since she'd never fired a gun before, but he had his weapon. A big one.

She held her breath as Riley tinkered with the sliding door, slicing out a portion of the glass with a glass cutter. When the door slid open without a clanging alarm bell sounding, Amy released her breath in a gush of air.

They stepped into the kitchen where circles of lights from the various gadgets and kitchen appliances winked at them from the darkness. The ice maker cranked, and Amy clutched Riley's arm.

He looked at her over his shoulder, raising his eyebrows to the folded edge of his knit cap.

She released her death grip and shrugged as if ice makers terrified her every day.

They tiptoed from the kitchen into the great room where a shaft of light from the entryway beamed across the carpet. An empty chair stood sentry in the foyer and Riley's brow furrowed as he pointed toward it.

Amy gulped. Looked like a good place for a bodyguard to stand watch but, if the bodyguard wasn't occupying the chair, where was he?

Riley placed one gloved hand on the banister of the curving staircase while his other hovered over the gun in his waistband. He tested the first step with his running shoe, and meeting no resistance or creaking, he began his ascent.

Amy trailed after him, keeping watch behind them. She didn't want some thug to come barreling out of the shadows. On the one hand, she wanted to find Ethan home and tucked into his bed so they could question him and get the heck out of here. On the other, she dreaded the encounter and wanted more time to shore up her nerves while they waited for him to come home.

Several rooms lined the hallway upstairs, most with their doors gaping open. The lights they'd seen from outside spilled from two rooms next to each other, their doors ajar.

Would they find Ethan reading quietly in bed? It seemed so out of character for him, and the eerie silence of the house indicated emptiness. Surely they'd hear a cough, the rustle of a page, the clinking of a glass if Ethan occupied one of those rooms.

Riley held a hand out behind him as he crept down the hallway, gripping his weapon in front of him. Her muscles stiff with tension, Amy followed behind him.

Grabbing the doorjamb of the first room, Riley poked his head through the doorway. His shoulders stiffened and the muscles of his back beneath his black T-shirt rippled.

He cranked his head over his shoulder and mouthed, "Wait here."

Amy's blood thundered in her ears. Ethan must be in there, but he obviously hadn't spotted Riley yet. He had to be sleeping.

Riley disappeared into the room and panic washed over Amy's flesh. She tripped toward the door and grasped the doorjamb. The king-sized bed looked like a raft afloat in the ocean in the cavernous bedroom decorated in dark blues and greens.

Riley's body blocked her view of Ethan, but a pair of bare feet pointed inward at the foot of the bed. Tilting her head, Amy drew her brows together. Ethan lay on top of the covers not beneath, so maybe he had fallen asleep reading.

Ethan hadn't yet made a noise. He'd have a nice surprise waking up with a big gun in his face. *Served him right.*

Riley leaned forward, his weapon dangling at his side. Amy scratched her head beneath the cap and sighed as she drew closer to the bed.

Riley spun around with his arms splayed at his sides. "Stay where you are, Amy."

Did he think Ethan might wake up with guns blazing or something? She took a few more steps. Suddenly, her nose twitched, and then her nostrils flared. A sickening odor wafted from the bed, engulfing her, invading her nostrils and triggering her gag reflex. Her gut rolled as she clapped a hand over her mouth.

She staggered back and hissed. "What is that?"

Riley stepped to the side, revealing Ethan's prone form on the bed. Amy's gaze traveled the length of Ethan's body, clothed in a blue silk dressing gown splashed with red and black. Her examination ended with his white feet, toes oddly pointing inward.

Something nudged her brain and her eyes shifted direction, gaining focus as she scanned Ethan's robe with its strange color pattern. She studied his face, his eyes closed and his head resting against a pillow, a pillow soaked in blood.

Chapter Twelve

Amy screamed, the sound ripping through the room and banishing the silence in the house. The scream died in her throat and she gathered breath for another one, her gaze pinned to the deep slash across Ethan's throat.

Riley lunged forward and pulled her into his arms. He cupped the back of her head with his hand and crushed her face against his T-shirt, now damp with sweat. She inhaled his masculine scent, anything to get the rancid smell of blood and death out of her nose.

He shushed her. "Quiet, Amy. They might still be here."

His words sent a spike of fear to her heart, and she bucked in his arms.

He clasped one arm around her waist and half dragged her toward the door while thrusting his gun before him. He stalked to the other lighted room, peered inside and cursed.

Amy peeled her head from his shoulder, but he clamped it back down. "You don't need to see that."

She licked her lips, her tongue meeting his rough T-shirt. She didn't need to see whatever lurked in that room, but she prayed to God Ethan didn't have a family.

"We need to get out of here." He squeezed her shoulder. "Are you okay to walk?"

She jerked her head up. Did Riley think he needed to carry her away from the carnage? She realized she hadn't stood on her own two feet since she saw Ethan's body. She steadied her rubbery legs and drew a deep breath. "I'm okay."

Still holding his gun, Riley grabbed her hand and charged downstairs. They flew across the great room, burst through the sliding door of the kitchen, and stumbled into the backyard. Their soft shoes squished against the damp grass as they made a beeline toward the foliage ringing the yard.

They scrambled through the bushes and hopped over the fence of the next-door neighbors. Amy had been so worried on the way over about meeting a pit bull in this yard; now she'd take on five pit bulls just to get away from that grisly scene in the house.

When they made it to Riley's car, they both sat panting in the front seat. Amy's heart pounded in her chest like she'd just made an ocean rescue. Except this time she hadn't rescued anybody.

She gripped her bouncing knees with gloved hands. "Riley, what was in that other room? N-not his family?"

He slipped off his cap and bunched it in his fist. "No, thank God. His bodyguards—two of them."

Amy choked and covered her face. "Why?"

"His attackers must've figured he knew something." His fingers inched inside her cap and massaged her scalp. "I'm sorry you had to see that."

She peeked through her fingers, the streetlights blurring through her tears. "Do you think Ethan told them anything? Maybe he did know where Carlos stashed the money. If so…"

"If so, then they'll have what they want and leave you alone."

"And if Ethan didn't know anything, they killed him anyway. I don't know anything." Amy pulled off her gloves and hugged herself against the cold fear that touched the base of her spine.

"They won't get to you, Amy. I won't let them."

She met his eyes and, even in the darkness of the car, she could see the fierce protective light gleaming from their depths. Dropping her eyelids, she rolled her shoulders. She had faith in Riley.

He picked up her hand and traced the lines of her palm with his fingertip. "I think it's time for you to leave."

She curled her hand around his finger. "Okay. Let's go back to your place. Should we call the police or something?"

"I have someone I can call at the sheriff's department. I know Ethan's your brother, Amy, but the police aren't going to be choked up over his death." He slipped his hand from hers and cranked on the car's engine.

"He wasn't a good person, even as a teenager. I suppose the authorities will notify Dad. I'm not going to be the one to tell him his favored son is dead."

"I'm sure your father will be notified. It'll be reported as just another murder due to drug trafficking."

"Now I'll never get any information from Ethan. I hope his killers had better luck and they have what they want now. Otherwise, we're back to square one trying to figure out where Carlos hid that money."

"Didn't you hear me?" Riley cocked his head as he took the next turn.

"You think Ethan gave it up?"

"No, not that. I said you need to leave."

Her nostrils flared as she studied his profile, the ends of his long, sandy blond hair highlighted by the headlights from the oncoming cars. "You mean *leave* leave?"

"Yeah. Leave the area. Where's that EMT school you were going to attend?"

"Right here in San Diego." She sat up and yanked off the itchy cap. "Where do you propose I go and for how long? If the client never gets his money back, they'll never leave me alone. What am I supposed to do, join the Witness Protection Program?" She slammed her hands against the dashboard. "I already went through a similar experience when I was ten years old—uprooted, taken away from everything I'd ever known and loved, thrust into an alien environment. I'm not doing that again."

He brushed her cheek with the back of his hand. "It won't be like that, Amy. I can send you to stay with a friend, Ian's ex-wife in Colorado. They wouldn't be able to track you there. When all this blows over..."

"How's that going to happen?" She ducked out of his reach. "Carlos left the means to that money with me, somehow, somewhere. How are you going to find it without my help? And if you never find it, they'll never stop looking for me. I don't want to permanently settle in Colorado. I don't like the snow."

Tears pricked her eyes, and she turned her head to rest her forehead against the cool glass of the window. She'd been an idiot to expect Riley to whisk her away to his dive boat in Cabo. The excitement and the thrill of the chase had fueled his attraction for her. Nothing more. Maybe he wanted to prove to himself that he could protect someone and do it right this time.

And what did she want to prove?

She'd been fooling herself all these years thinking she could settle down with a stable man—no excitement, no drama. Then this situation had fallen into her lap like a ripe fruit, and she'd grabbed it with both hands and sunk her teeth into it.

Riley swung into his parking slot and cut the engine. "I have to call my friend at the San Diego Sheriff's Department to report that carnage."

"Will you tell him the truth?"

"As much as I can. Ethan Prescott was involved in a drug deal that took a wrong turn, and he paid with his life."

After they'd locked the doors behind them in Riley's apartment, Amy watched Riley end his call to the sheriff's department. "No questions asked?"

He shook his head as he pocketed his phone. "That was my contact, Walt. He's a former Navy SEAL and he doesn't ask questions."

"Why'd they do it, Riley?" Amy twisted her fingers in front of her. "Why would a bunch of terrorists kill Ethan?"

"He was involved in the drug trade. He had bodyguards living in his house. He knew the risks."

"But the day before he was throwing a dinner party. It doesn't seem as if he was in fear for his life."

"Then he was a fool."

Amy pressed the heels of her hands against her temples. "Do you think they killed him because of me?"

"What do you mean?" Riley shifted his gaze away from her to study the newspaper on the counter.

For a covert ops guy, his lying skills needed work. "Come on. Don't pretend with me. Do you think the terrorists went after Ethan to find me?"

He folded the newspaper, running his thumb along the crease. "They probably don't even know about the relationship between the two of you. But they probably do know about his connection to Carlos. When he couldn't tell them anything about the money, they killed him."

"If Ethan had known where Carlos had hidden the money, he would've told them. My half brother had a keen sense of self-preservation."

Riley snorted. "Most criminals do." He took two steps toward her and grabbed her hands. "Put it behind you, Amy. Get some sleep. You've had a shock today."

"That's three dead bodies in as many days." A half smile trembled on her lips. "That's gotta be some kind of record."

He cradled her face in his large, comforting hands. "That's too much for anyone to bear. You need to get out of this, and I'm going to help you."

"Before you do that, can you help me with one more thing?" She turned her head to kiss his palm, fluttering her lashes against his fingers. She wasn't above using her feminine wiles to get her way.

"Anything." He dropped a kiss on top of her head.

"Get me in to see my father tomorrow."

He gasped against the top of her head, a gush of warm air hitting her scalp. "Why do you want to see your father? The police will notify him of Ethan's death."

"Now that I know Ethan was responsible for involving

me in a crime, I want to find out what else my father knows about it. Maybe Ethan confided in him about Carlos. Maybe my father has some ideas about the money."

"I thought you'd given up on finding the money." Riley gripped Amy's shoulders and pushed her away, intently studying her upturned face.

"*You* gave up on finding the money. I never agreed to that, Riley. I want to find it, turn it over to the proper authorities and get my life back."

"What if it doesn't work?" His fingers pinched into her flesh through the black sweatshirt. He continued, his tone harsh, his words brutal. "What if you find their money, turn it over, and they kill you as a reward for your efforts?"

She hunched her shoulders, twisting out of his grasp. "That was supposed to make me feel better? That's your way of protecting me?"

"That's my way of talking sense into you. Don't play this game with terrorists, Amy. You'll lose."

"Even with the all-powerful Navy SEAL, Riley Hammond, at my side? You said you'd protect me from anything." Amy ground her teeth together after the childish words tumbled from her mouth. Riley had hurt her by not offering to take her back to Cabo with him, and now she wanted to hurt him in return.

"I will, Amy." He dragged her back against his chest, wrapping his arms around her body like a protective shield. The stubble on his chin caught the strands of her hair. "God knows, I will protect you from anything and anyone. That's why I want you out of here."

She sagged against him. "Do this one thing for me, Riley. It's not a regular visiting day tomorrow, but you can get me in. Do it and I'll leave San Diego. I'll go anywhere you want."

Especially Cabo.

He hugged her tighter. "I'll get you in to see your father tomorrow and when he doesn't come through for you, we'll get you the hell out of Dodge."

She turned in his embrace, wrapped her arms around his neck and pressed her cheek against the steady, sure beating of his heart. She'd made a promise and she'd stick to it, but if her father gave her information—the game changed.

RILEY HADN'T SURPRISED the warden at the San Miguel Federal Pen with his request to visit Eli Prescott. They'd already gotten word of Ethan's murder. The warden figured Riley's visit might be part of the ongoing investigation. Riley felt no inclination to correct the warden's impression.

He glanced at Amy in the seat next to him, humming and tapping her sandaled feet together to the beat of the music on the radio. The sight of Ethan with his throat slit had done her in last night, but she'd made a miraculous recovery. Nothing fazed this woman for long. She had the resiliency of a rubber band.

He pitied her for it.

She must've endured a lot as a kid to have built up that hardened shell. She needed his protection less than he cared to admit to himself. But she did need his contacts, and he'd been happy to accommodate her—especially since she'd agreed to leave town.

"So what's on the agenda?"

"What?" She turned her large, liquid brown eyes on

him and he wondered how old Eli Prescott could refuse her anything. He sure as hell couldn't.

"What do you plan to ask your father?"

Her brows shot up. "The obvious. Did he know Carlos? Does he know about the money?"

"And even if he does, why should he tell you?"

She blinked her eyes rapidly. "To save my life."

He opened his mouth and then snapped it shut. He didn't need to explain her father's character to Amy. He couldn't help her if she refused to open her eyes.

She laughed, a hard, bitter sound. "I know what you're thinking. Why should he care about me now? Granted, if it came down to choosing between his life and mine, his choice would be a slam dunk. But if he could help me without hurting himself, he just might sign up for that."

"And you're okay with that?"

"I have to be." She lifted a shoulder and her long hair slid forward. "It's all I've got."

He made the turn onto the property of the prison and pointed to the right. "We have to park over there today since they're holding some kind of event in the administration building and the prison is closed to visitors."

He pulled his car into a slot near the front and cupped Amy's elbow as they strode toward the gate that led to the prison.

The guard checked their IDs. "Good thing you came early. That lot's going to fill up, and we're not letting anyone past the gates later today."

"What's going on?" Riley glanced back at a news van trundling up the drive.

"Warden's having a press conference."

Riley thanked the guard and threaded his fingers

through Amy's as they walked toward the imposing gray penitentiary. "Are you nervous?"

"No more nervous than usual when I visit him. He always wants to talk about the good old days, and I'm always asking questions." She squeezed his hand. "Thanks for getting me in here today."

He squeezed back. "*No problemo,* but a promise is a promise."

"Colorado? I may need to buy a warm jacket."

Since Riley had made the visit request, he had to accompany Amy into the visiting room. The warden had told him that Eli Prescott didn't rate visits beyond the glass partition, but Amy seemed accustomed to the routine.

She settled into the plastic chair opposite the bullet-proof glass and rested her hand on the red receiver. Riley took the seat to her right, his knees bumping hers.

The door beyond the glass swung open, and the guard ushered in a tall, lean man with cropped gray hair. Amy got her coloring from her mother but her body type from this man, this criminal.

Prescott dropped into the chair across from Amy and leveled a finger at Riley as he picked up the receiver. "Who's he?"

"He's just a friend."

Just a friend? God, he wanted to be so much more.

The blue eyes flickered across Riley's face, and Riley felt scanned and categorized in that split second.

"And they let him just waltz in here? Don't play games with me, girl." He coughed and covered his face with one bony hand. "You know I lost a son."

"Do you want to lose a daughter, too?"

Prescott jerked up his head. "What do you mean by that?"

"The same men who killed Ethan are after me." She gripped the edge of the counter in front of her. "Or don't you care about that?"

"It's that Carlos. If he had delivered the money to the clients as expected, Ethan would be alive and you'd be on the beach somewhere."

"What do you know about Carlos? What do you know about the money?" Amy had slid her hand to the glass where she splayed her fingers almost in supplication to her father.

His hand met hers through the glass. "I don't know anything, Amy."

Riley blew a slow stream of air through his teeth, unaware he'd been holding his breath.

"Ethan mentioned his deals to me occasionally but never the details. Why would he? How could I help him from here? How can I help you?"

Amy slumped in her seat, but kept her hand in place on the glass. "I—I don't know. These people think I have their money, and I don't have a clue where it is. They're not going to stop until they find out one way or the other if I have it."

"Then get out." Prescott's gaze shifted to Riley again. "I'm sure your capable friend here can find you a way out. People disappear all the time."

"I don't want to disappear. I'm always disappearing." Amy's voice never quavered for a second.

Her father tapped his nails on the glass. "I see you're still wearing your mother's locket. When did she give that to you?"

"Do you really want to know?" Amy's fingers curled

against the glass. "She gave it to me as she lay dying in the dirt of the compound under the hot Mexican sun. As the blood and life seeped from her body, she clasped it in her hand and told me to take it. To honor her last wish, I had to lift her heavy hair and slip the chain over her head…I had to take it off her dead body."

Prescott dropped his piercing blue gaze. "I loved Loretta and she loved me. I didn't keep her on the compound against her will, Amy, no matter how much you want to believe that."

Riley ached to take this brave woman into his arms and give her license to break down. But she'd never allow it, especially not in front of Eli Prescott.

Amy sighed, the only sound of her pent-up emotion. "Then you have nothing for me? You can't tell me anything about Carlos or the money he stole?"

"I wish I could. I really wish I could." His gaze brightened. "You've searched for keys? Numbers to bank accounts? Computer files?"

"We've searched."

Prescott put his hand back against the glass. "Stay safe, girl. You've got more gumption than all my other children put together. You always did."

Amy uncurled her fingers and pressed the glass. Then she dropped the receiver in its cradle and turned to Riley. "Let's go."

As they left the room, Riley glanced over his shoulder at the beaten man shuffling toward lockup on the other side of the glass. If Eli Prescott could've, he would've given Amy what she wanted—this time.

Amy's low heeled sandals clicked on the tiled floor as they walked down the hallway toward the reception area. The guards in the front were watching the event in the administration building on closed-circuit TVs.

"Is there a ladies' room in the administration building?"

"Yes." The guard at the desk nodded. "You'll probably have it all to yourself once this press conference gets underway."

Good. Amy needed a few minutes to herself.

"Are there any vending machines over there?" Riley slid his visitor's badge across the desk and Amy added hers.

"To the left once you enter the double doors."

Riley turned to Amy as they filed out of the prison into the bright sun. He skimmed his hand down her back, which she held stiff and straight. He figured she had to, or she might collapse into a puddle.

"Are you okay?"

Amy brushed the hair from her face and smiled a phony smile, too cheery for their surroundings. "I'm good."

"Do you want something to drink for the ride back?"

"Anything cold and wet." She fanned her legs with her skirt. "It's hot out here."

Riley pushed open the door of the stucco building, holding it for Amy. They waded through the crowd gathering before the podium at the end of the room. Riley vaguely remembered some news about a possible shutdown of the facility in the next few years. Maybe if they moved her father far, far away Amy would have a good excuse not to visit him anymore. Nothing but disappointment and heartache lurked behind those prison bars for her.

Amy pointed to the sign on the wall for the restrooms. "I'll meet you out front. It's a zoo in here."

Riley watched her as she turned the corner, her head held high and her silky hair rippling down her back. He spun around and collided with a reporter. The man's press badge fell to the floor, and Riley bent down to pick it up.

"Sorry." He glanced at the badge from KASD Radio before holding it out to the dark-haired man in the ill-fitting suit.

Sweat beaded the reporter's brow as he snatched at his badge. Without a word of thanks, the man turned toward the empty podium.

With irritation pricking the back of his neck, Riley muttered, "You're welcome," to the man's back and then made a beeline for the hallway to the left of the entrance.

He sauntered toward the bank of vending machines against the wall, jingling the change in his pocket. He clutched the coins and pulled them out, frowning as he added up the change in his palm. The red light on the soda machine indicated exact change only.

A woman in a pantsuit, her badge swaying from her neck, jogged toward the machine. She pointed to it. "Are you getting something?"

"I need exact change." He bounced the coins in his hand. "Do you have change for a couple of dollar bills?"

"I might. Hang on." She pinched open the coin purse on her wallet and stirred the change with her index finger.

"Sorry, I don't." She plucked out a few coins and fed them into the machine as her badge hung forward.

His brows drawing together, Riley studied her badge. KASD Radio, just like the other guy. They sure had a lot of press here for a little station and a little event.

Her soda chugged through the machine and clanged into the dispenser. "Ah-ha." She tapped the light on the machine. "It's your lucky day. I guess my change was enough to break the spell."

Riley dragged his gaze away from her badge—red, white and blue, instead of just red and white like the other reporter's—to stare stupidly at the machine where the red light had gone out.

"Are you okay? I think you can stuff your bills in there now."

Her wide eyes met his over the top of her soda can after she popped it open.

"Yeah, thanks." He scratched his jaw and stopped her as she turned away. "You're a reporter with KASD Radio?"

"Yep." She ran her thumb along the ribbon around her neck and held out her badge.

"I just ran into your colleague, literally. You're sure covering the warden's speech thoroughly. Is it that important?" He crumpled the bills in his fist, knowing the machine would never accept them now, but unable to curb the tension seizing his muscles.

She laughed. "I think you're mistaken. Our station doesn't have the budget to send two reporters to a news conference, even if the President himself showed up."

The blood roared in Riley's ears. "There's only you here from KASD?"

She nodded, taking a step back, the lines of her face creasing at the tone of his intense questioning.

"And this is the official badge for the event—red,

white and blue?" He grabbed her badge and tapped the hard plastic. The other badge had just been in a plastic sleeve.

She grabbed the ribbon and yanked the badge out of his hand. "What's your problem?"

The blood thrummed through his veins, and his sluggish senses began firing on all cylinders. He had a problem, all right. Amy was alone in the ladies' room and a rude reporter with suspicious credentials had free reign amidst a crowded building.

The big story here today had nothing to do with the warden. Amy was in trouble.

Chapter Thirteen

Amy stumbled as soon as she rounded the corner to the bathroom, and threw out her arm to steady herself against the wall.

The conversation with her father had leeched the strength from her bones—not because he couldn't tell her anything about the money, but because he hadn't remembered her mother had never removed the gold locket he'd given to his wife. Hadn't he realized Amy had taken the locket from her mother's dead body?

She clutched her stomach and staggered the rest of the way down the empty hallway to the bathroom. She shoved open the door and peered beneath the stalls. Good, she had the place to herself.

Gripping the sink for support, she peered into the mirror. Despite the turmoil of her emotions, her face stared back at her, placid and serene. She'd gotten so good at hiding her feelings, no wonder Riley hadn't invited her to Cabo. He probably had no idea how much she wanted to stay with him.

She cranked on the faucet and splashed cold water on her face. It didn't help. Nausea swept over her, and she swung around and stumbled into one of the stalls.

She slid the lock and leaned against the door, laying her hands flat against it.

She scooped in a deep breath and shuddered as she released it. Fresh air would do her more good than the stale, artificially perfumed air of the bathroom. The sooner they hit the road, the better. She closed her eyes and breathed deeply through her nose until the nausea passed.

The outer door to the bathroom whisked open as Amy yanked a length of toilet tissue from the roll and pressed it against her lips. The person who had opened that door gave her further incentive to buck up and fight off the sickness. She didn't want anyone to hear her retching in the bathroom.

She blew her nose into the tissue and tossed it into the toilet. After flushing, she slid back the lock and took two steps toward the sink. The woman in the other stall hadn't made a peep yet. Who knows? Maybe she was suppressing her nausea, too. The federal pen could make anyone ill.

The stall door banged open and Amy jumped. Her gaze darted to the reflection in the mirror—the reflection of a knife blade glinting in the fluorescent light.

Her blood turned to ice water in her veins as the face behind the knife came into focus. A stranger, a man who wanted to kill her.

"W-what do you want? I don't have the money. I don't know what Carlos did with the money."

The man wiped his brow with his other hand, and his eye twitched. "You're coming with me."

A pounding dread beat against her temples. If they believed she knew something, what would they do to her to get answers? She clutched her purse against her side. How would he manage to abduct her in the midst of the crowd, even if he did poke that knife in her side? If she made a run for it, would he stab her in front of all those people?

Riley would never allow him to just walk away with her. But if he had her at knifepoint, would Riley make a move?

"I have nothing to give you. No money, no information."

The man glanced over his shoulder at the door and ran the tip of his tongue along his lips. "Who is the man who travels with you and protects you? CIA?"

She swallowed. Maybe she did have information to give them. The image of Ethan's slashed throat and blood-soaked pillow flashed in front of her eyes. What information had he given them? Whatever it was, it hadn't been enough, and she knew a lot less than Ethan.

He gestured with his knife. "Let's get moving."

"You don't really believe you can march me off the grounds of a Federal prison during a press conference with a knife in my side, do you?"

"I have to do what I have to do." A bead of sweat rolled down his face and hung off the edge of his jaw.

He didn't like this any better than she did.

She shuffled back a few steps, but he lunged at her, grabbing the back of her neck with his free hand.

He pressed the blade against her side and growled. "Walk next to me. If you make a move or cry out, I'm going to slide this blade right into your flesh."

Her teeth chattered and goose bumps raced across her skin. Her hip glanced off the door as he pushed it open and looked both ways down the hallway.

Instead of turning left toward the murmuring crowd, the man veered to the right, his fist pressed against the small of her back and the blade pinching her side.

Her breath came out in short gasps. He had no intention of walking her through the crowd and possibly past Riley. There must be a back door to this place, and the guards didn't have to be as alert since the main gates to the prison remained locked.

A woman's voice called down the hallway to them. "Is this the way to the ladies' room?"

Amy craned her head over her shoulder and felt the blade poke her skin through her blouse. "Yes, that's it, on the right. We're leaving now. Enjoy the event."

"Shut up." The man drove his balled-up hand into her back.

Amy's too-familiar response didn't make the woman stop or ask if they knew each other. When they reached the end of the hallway, her captor pushed her toward an exit door at the bottom of a short staircase.

She had to make some kind of move. She coiled her muscles and jumped over the three steps, crashing into the metal door. She shoved against the bar on the door and tripped outside. But her assailant tackled her to the ground and held the knife to her throat.

"Don't be foolish again. I don't have orders to kill you, but I can cause you severe pain."

She swallowed against the blade and nodded as he dragged her to her feet. The exit door had deposited them at the side of the building with the open-air parking lot stretching to their left.

Amy cast a wild glance around for Riley or some prison guards, but spotted only a few reporters smoking cigarettes at the corner of the building. They weren't even looking her way.

The man hustled her toward the parking lot, gaining confidence with each step away from the prison. They weaved through the parked cars, the knife a constant reminder of the threat that faced her.

She wouldn't get in the car with him. She'd fight him off with every ounce of strength she had. He'd already confessed that he didn't have permission to kill her.

But he could do a lot worse with that wicked silver blade.

He reached into his pocket and clicked his remote. The lights of a nondescript gray sedan flashed from its parking space at the end of a row.

He yanked open the driver's door and pushed her ahead of him, the knife at her back. "Crawl over to the passenger seat. And don't think about exiting that way. It's impossible."

She looked across the interior of the car, zeroing in on the stripped panel of the passenger door. No door handle, no way to open the door.

Tensing her muscles, she gulped. She'd have to make her move now. He'd cut her now, or he'd cut her later, after she gave them unsatisfactory answers to their questions. Might as well make his life as miserable as possible.

She settled one knee on the car seat, bracing her other leg on the ground, ready to kick back. A scrambling noise behind them caused them both to freeze, and then her attacker grunted and tumbled to the side.

Amy twisted around, landing on the driver's seat, her legs splayed before her. Both fear and relief spiraled through her body as she saw Riley bend over the man and punch him in the gut.

The man groped for his knife, which he'd dropped at Riley's initial onslaught.

She screamed, "Look out. He has a knife."

Riley dropped onto the man's body, pinning his wrist with his knee. "Run, Amy. Get out of here."

She had no intention of leaving Riley in this parking lot with a madman. Turning toward the steering wheel, she laid on the horn with both hands.

The stranger, knife in hand, swiped across Riley's midsection, ripping his shirt. With his other hand, he grabbed Amy's ankle and yanked her from the car. She gripped the steering wheel, hanging on, her palms sweaty.

Riley scrambled to his hands and knees, and the stranger kicked him in the throat. As Riley grunted and tumbled to the side, Amy's attacker launched forward, landing on top of her and waving his knife in her face.

Riley swayed to his feet. "I'm not going to let you take her."

With Amy crushed beneath his weight, the man brought the knife to her throat. Riley cursed and froze. He wouldn't make a move if he feared the man would cut her.

Amy took a deep breath and twisted her head away from the knife, ducking beneath the steering column. He yanked her hair and nicked her shoulder with the knife as he tried to pull her head back onto the seat.

Blood dripped onto the console. Amy gasped, but she worked an arm free and cinched the man's wrist, digging her nails into his flesh until he hissed in pain.

Riley threw open the passenger door and hooked one

arm around her, dragging her from the car as he elbowed her attacker in the temple. With his knife still clutched in his hand, the man lunged toward them.

Amy jerked her head up at the sound of boots on the pavement. Two guards from the prison shouted as they jogged toward them.

Their assailant shoved them the rest of the way out of the car and gunned the engine. The car lurched forward, the passenger door slamming shut from the force of the forward motion. Exhaust filled Amy's nostrils as Riley yanked her out of the way of the tires grappling for purchase on the asphalt. He covered her body and rolled to the side.

The car squealed out of the parking lot and flew over the speed bumps, and Amy looked up to see it careen onto the road leading off the prison grounds.

With hands hovering over their weapons, the guards approached Amy and Riley. Amy slumped against Riley, panting against his chest. Riley hugged her close, murmuring in her ear. Her blood soaked through his shirt, and he must've felt the moisture because he glanced down and sucked in a breath.

"You're hurt."

"I'm all right. It's not deep."

He was already ripping off his shirt when the guards arrived, looming above them. "What the hell happened here?"

Riley staunched the bleeding of her arm with his shirt, and then squinted up at the prison guards. "It's a long story."

"Do you think anyone believed that terrorists infiltrated the press corps at the prison and tried to kidnap me?"

Riley lifted a shoulder. "It doesn't matter one way or the other. It's not as if a bunch of Federal prison guards are going to track down terrorist operatives."

"At least they didn't arrest us for fighting in the parking lot."

She carried a glass of water to the couch and sank against the cushions. Riley had explained to her about the suspicious reporter and his badge, and how he had rushed to the ladies' room to find her. That woman in the hallway had saved Amy and didn't even know it. When Riley had stopped her coming out of the bathroom, she'd pointed down the corridor and told him about the chatty woman and the surly man.

Smacking his fist into his palm, Riley said, "I should've stopped at my car first and retrieved my weapon."

"If you had done that, it might've been too late."

"Maybe. I just didn't want the guy to see me in the parking lot. I crouched down between the cars the whole time I was tracking you. I didn't want to take my eyes off of you for a second."

"I'm glad you didn't." Riley was turning into her guardian angel, and did she ever need one.

"How's your shoulder?" He swept his beer from the counter and twisted off the cap.

"It's fine." Amy picked at the snowy-white bandage peeping from the collar of her shirt. "They've moved onto the next step, haven't they? That man tried to kidnap me today. They're going to find out what I know, whether I know it or not."

Riley sauntered into the living room and slumped on the couch next to her, holding up his bottle. "Sure you don't want one? If ever someone needed a drink, it's you."

"I need my wits about me." Her knee bounced, and she hunched forward on her elbows to stop it.

"Those aren't wits. Those are nerves." He ran his hand between her shoulder blades. "Besides, you don't need wits anymore. You're getting out of town, remember?"

"You don't have to persuade me." She shivered, and Riley massaged her neck.

The attempted kidnapping today had convinced her to leave. Maybe fate dictated that she pull up her roots every ten years or so and move on. Her future didn't include hearth and home or stable and serene. She shot Riley a sideways glance.

And it didn't look like her future would include him either.

"Good because I'm just about done persuading you." He sipped his beer. "My next plan included throwing you over my shoulder."

Closing her eyes, Amy leaned against him, soaking up his strength. She wouldn't mind that at all. If she could trust this man with her life, she could trust him with her heart.

He slipped an arm around her. "Does Colorado sound good? There's no snow there—yet."

She dropped her head on his shoulder, allowing her hair to fan across her face. "Cabo sounds better, and there's no snow there—ever."

His body stiffened, and she held her breath. Had she gone too far? After today's rescue, she'd decided to tell him exactly how she felt. She'd weathered many calamities in her life. She could handle a broken heart.

"Cabo?"

"That's where you live, isn't it?" She flattened her hand against his belly. "Unless you've been lying to me all this time. Do you really own a dive boat in Mexico?"

"Yes, but…"

"But what?" Her confidence and resolve evaporated. She pushed away from him and jumped up from the couch. "This is just a job? It's in your nature to protect a damsel in distress? You only slept with me to make me feel better?"

She clenched her teeth, curling her hands into fists, bracing for the rejection, feeling foolish that she'd set herself up.

"But I'm not done with this job yet."

Amy blinked. "What does that mean?"

"I was called out of retirement to find my friend, Jack Coburn. The trail started with the Velasquez Drug Cartel and its deal with a terrorist cell from Afghanistan. I have to find out how they plan to use that money. It might lead to Jack and it might not, but right now it's all we have. When the job is done, when Jack is safe, then I can think about the future."

Looking down, her hair creating a veil around her face, Amy asked, "What's in your future, Riley?"

The couch squeaked as he rose. His body heat warmed her skin as he stood inches away from her. His scent, fresh soap and a hint of the sea—always a hint of the sea—flooded her senses.

He cupped his hand at the ends of her hair, her dark strands pooling in his palm. Then he scooped her hair away from her face into a ponytail behind her, tugging on it so her head tilted back, her face exposed to his scrutiny.

"Don't you know what's in my future, Amy?"

A gleam of blue shone from under his half-lidded eyes and his lips quirked at one side. She trailed her fingers along the reddish-gold stubble of his chin and whispered, "Me?"

He kissed her fingertips. He kissed the bandage on her shoulder. He kissed her mouth.

"It took you only one guess. I thought I'd have a tougher time convincing you of my intentions than getting you to leave San Diego."

"What exactly are your intentions?" She tugged on his earlobe and tucked his long hair behind his ear.

He rolled his eyes. "You still have doubts?"

"I'll always have doubts, Riley. Is that going to drive you crazy?"

He nuzzled her neck. "You already drive me crazy."

"I'm serious." She cradled his head with her arms. "Will my insecurities wear you down?"

"You're not going to have any insecurities with me. I'm not going anywhere, Amy. I won't abandon you."

She murmured against his hair, soft and damp from his shower. "What if I abandon you?"

"I'll come after you. It'll give me a good excuse to throw you over my shoulder." He kissed her hands and pulled her back toward the couch. "You do have to abandon me for a while though. Let's get Ian's ex-wife, Meg, on the phone and see if she can take you in."

After two unsuccessful calls to Meg's house and her work, Riley tapped his phone against his palm. "Rocky Mountain Adventures, the place where Meg works, told me Meg's on vacation."

Amy's pulse ticked faster. Once she'd decided to leave town, she couldn't wait to get out even if that meant leaving Riley behind. He'd come for her when this ended, when he found his friend.

"That's okay. I can find someplace to stay. I still have a lot of money at my disposal."

He shook his head. "I don't want you staying alone. I can send you to my sister and her husband in Hawaii. You'd get along great with them. They own a surf shop and spend most of the day surfing and hanging out at the beach."

"Do you come from a laid-back family? Surf shops in Hawaii. Dive boats in Cabo. What prompted you to enlist in the navy?"

"My dad was not laid-back—anything but. He was an admiral in the navy and ran our household like a tight ship. My sister, Leah, rebelled against all of that. I followed in Dad's footsteps, and then decided my sister had the right idea."

"Except when it comes to rescuing friends."

"Except that."

"Where are your parents now?"

"My mother remarried after my father died. She lives in Florida. My dad died of a heart attack at sixty-two. That's what being a type A personality gets you."

She folded her legs beneath her. Riley had two sides pulling at him. Maybe that's why they'd hit it off so quickly. They'd each recognized a kindred spirit. "A type A personality also allows you to control your destiny. I don't think you would've been satisfied kicking back in Cabo all your life. Your father wouldn't have been either."

"You're right." He tugged her hair. "When the call

came from Colonel Scripps about Jack, I jumped at the chance. I told myself I was responding to a friend in need, but I was also responding to my own need—my need for excitement, thrills and chills."

"I think it's also your need to feel useful, Riley, to have a hand in carving fate. Even your marriage to April was a challenge."

His nostrils flared briefly. *Have I gone too far?* She treaded on hallowed ground whenever she mentioned his marriage.

He blew out a breath and slid open his cell phone. "Sister in Hawaii? Does that work for you?"

"Will it work for her?"

"I told you she takes things in stride. She won't even raise an eyebrow."

After a conversation during which Riley seemed to do all the talking with very little explaining, he tossed his phone onto the coffee table. "Done. We'll put you on a flight tomorrow, and you can give Leah a call when you get there."

"You didn't tell her much."

"She knows not to ask too many questions." He clicked his beer on the table. "Are you ready to turn in?"

She set her water glass on the table next to his half-empty bottle. "It's our last night together. How…? When…?"

"We'll be together again when my job is done." He pinched her chin, and she closed her eyes.

She'd be safe in Hawaii, and he'd still be chasing terrorists and drug dealers, facing danger every day. But he wouldn't have it any other way, and she'd have to stand by that. She'd have to respect his commitment to finding his friend.

After all, that's what she loved about him. Why she loved him.

She covered his hand with hers. She'd never been in love before—never had the courage—and now, she didn't have the courage to tell him. Not even knowing she had to leave him.

His warm breath caressed her cheek and he kissed her eyelids. "I'm not going to waste this night worrying. I can finally relax knowing you're with my sister and her husband and away from this threat."

She opened one eye. "My involvement has complicated everything, hasn't it?"

"Only in a good way." Standing up, he extended his hand toward her. "Let's turn in, together. One last night with you, and I'll be highly motivated to wrap up this job."

Giggling, she placed her hand in his. She could forget her troubles for a while—as long as they made love. As long as he held her in his arms.

Her phone played its ringtone from her purse, and she squeezed Riley's hand. "Hold that thought. I hope this isn't Sarah. I'll have to tell her I abandoned her house."

She groped for the cell phone inside her purse and studied the unfamiliar number on the display. Her heart skipped a beat, and she caught her breath.

"Who is it?"

"Don't know. Could be the EMT school, but probably not at this time of night."

She punched the button to answer. "Hello?"

"*Mi amor.* I've missed you."

The blood rushed to Amy's head, and she flung out a hand to grab the arm of the chair. "Who is this?"

"It's Carlos. I'm coming for you."

Chapter Fourteen

Her face drained of its usual bronze glow, Amy dropped the phone and collapsed onto the chair. A man's voice squawked from the phone and Riley pinched it between his fingers and mouthed to Amy. "Who is it?"

She opened her mouth and emitted a croak. Then she cleared her throat and tried again. "Carlos."

Riley nearly dropped the phone a second time. Her dead ex-boyfriend? His mind raced. Who said he was dead? The so-called body vanished, and Amy had never given him a chance to check the man's pulse. They hadn't seen any blood, and Riley had seen no visible wounds.

He put his finger to his lips and pressed the speaker button on Amy's phone. Cradling the phone in his palm, he held out his hand to her.

A golden opportunity just dropped into their laps. Could she do this? Did he have a right to ask her?

Slowly she nodded and took the phone from him. She scooped in a shaky breath. "C-Carlos?"

He laughed. "That's right, *mi amor*. Did you think I was dead?"

"I saw you on my kitchen floor, Carlos. What happened?"

"I took a pill, a drug. Something that slowed my heart rate, paralyzed me. Unless a doctor examined me, I appeared as good as dead."

Covert ops guys carried those kinds of drugs in their arsenal. Carlos had been prepared for anything. The shock of discovering her ex-boyfriend alive and well and on the telephone hadn't worn off for Amy yet.

Riley tapped her shoulder and mouthed, *Why?*

She blinked her eyes. "Why, Carlos? Why would you take something like that?"

"It has its dangers, Amy, but nothing compared to the threats of terrorist scum. When I knew they followed me to your house, I swallowed a little blow pill and faked my death. I didn't know if they'd figure it out and kill me anyway, but I had to take the chance."

Riley twirled his finger in the air. She had to get as much out of Carlos as possible while he was still alive.

"I thought they'd come to my house and removed your body."

"No. I came to and walked out of your house. I knew you'd been there because I saw a wet suit on the floor, unless that belonged to the clients or Velazquez's men. I'm pretty sure both were after me when I didn't deliver the money."

Amy closed her eyes, the color gradually returning to her cheeks. "Why'd you do it, Carlos? Why did you double-cross them all?"

"Surely you know, *mi amor.*"

"I don't know, and please don't…"

She trailed off as Riley drew his finger across his throat. No sense in angering Carlos at this point. They needed him.

"Please don't tell me I know. I haven't seen you in a few months. Do you even have a wife?"

Carlos chuckled. "Of course not. How could there be anyone for me but you? When you accused me of being married, I figured it was a good way to draw back until I pulled off this deal."

"Why, Carlos?"

"I wanted the money for us, Amy. We can go away now, be together."

Amy's eyes widened and she swallowed. "B-be together?"

Riley bunched his fists, but he nodded. Carlos had the money, and Riley needed to get his hands on it.

"You and me, *mi amor*. You need someone to take care of you."

Her gaze slid to Riley, and he rubbed her thigh. *She has someone to take care of her.*

She blew out a long, silent breath. "Why did you come back to my place after the deal went bad?"

"To get the money and to get you."

"Where's the money, Carlos?"

Riley held his breath.

"The money is in a self-storage facility. I got the idea from that storage shed on the beach."

"So why come to my place to get the money?"

"I left the key with you." He coughed. "I didn't think it would put you in danger. I couldn't keep it myself in case I was captured."

"You didn't think it would put me in danger?" Amy ran her hands through her hair, clutching it at her scalp. "They figured you were at my house for a reason. They're after me now."

"I know that, *mi amor. Lo siento.* I had no idea they'd put things together so quickly."

Amy massaged her left temple with her fingertips. "Where did you leave the key?"

Carlos drew in a sharp breath, and Riley held Amy's dark gaze, still glassy with shock.

"Come to me. Come to me and we'll get the money together and then sail away."

Riley rolled his eyes. Was this guy for real? Carlos didn't know Amy if he thought that kind of amour talk would work with her.

From his crouching position, Riley pushed up and paced toward the window. It had just ended. Carlos wouldn't tell Amy where he'd hidden the key to the storage container unless he got Amy in the bargain. Of course, Carlos wouldn't get the money either.

"Where do you want me to meet you?"

Riley spun around and stalked to Amy's side. He held up his hands and shook his head.

She ignored him. "I'll come to you anywhere, Carlos."

Carlos sighed a noisy, wet sigh, and Riley grunted. Was he crying now?

"I knew it wasn't the end. I knew you wouldn't give up on us. Meet me at the marina tomorrow at seven in the evening, slip eight-fifteen."

The guy wasn't kidding about sailing away.

"Do I need to bring anything? How will you know I have the key with me?"

"Let me worry about that. I know what to do. Just pack a bag." Carlos paused. "You'll come alone, won't you? This isn't some kind of trick? You won't show up with the police?"

Amy finally made eye contact with Riley. "No trick. I'll be there alone."

"Until tomorrow, *mi amor.*"

"Until tomorrow."

Amy slid her phone shut and Riley snatched it to view the number. "Probably a prepaid phone." He fired her cell phone at the couch and it hit the cushion and bounced to the floor. "What do you think you're doing?"

"I'm meeting Carlos tomorrow, and we're going to get that money." She stood up and stretched, tousling her hair. "Once you get the money, you can halt the terrorists' plans and maybe get some information about Jack."

He surveyed her through narrowed eyes. "How do you plan to get the money from Lover Boy?"

"You just said it. Lover Boy. I'll get Carlos to do what I want one way or another."

"You're crazy. He's a criminal. He had the nerve to double-cross a terrorist cell and the Velasquez boys. He's not going to kowtow to you for the sake of love."

"You never know."

"You're not going alone."

"If he sees you, he'll run."

"He won't see me." He pulled her into his arms. "If you're going through with this insane plan, I'm going to be by your side...*mi amor.*"

Amy placed her hands on either side of his face and drew him down for a hard kiss on the mouth. "Don't call me that—ever."

THE FOLLOWING DAY after hours of planning, Amy sipped her coffee as Riley outlined plans and escape routes on a legal pad for the hundredth time. "I don't want you getting into a boat, plane or automobile with Carlos."

Amy tipped more milk into her cup. "I'm kinda gonna have to if we want to find the money. You'll be following us anyway, right? And maybe we'll get lucky, and Carlos and I will use my car."

He tapped a small metal disk on the counter for the umpteenth time. "I think we should use the bug. Even if Carlos suspects you, he won't be able to detect this if we tuck it in your waistband."

"Are you trying to convince me or yourself? I already told you—I'm game."

"If Carlos discovers it…"

"He's not going to discover it. How else am I supposed to let you know where we're going? If you're going to be watching us from some concealed location or from far away, what am I supposed to do, send up smoke signals?"

"I can always follow you at a discreet distance. He won't detect me, and we'll have the GPS on your car just in case." He cupped his hand and bounced the little listening device up and down in his palm.

Riley had more jitters than a Thoroughbred at the starting gates of the Kentucky Derby. She laid her hand flat against his, trapping the disc. "If he won't discover you following us, he's not going to find this little microphone on my body or in my clothes. Hook that baby up."

The deep lines between his eyebrows didn't budge, but he nodded. "I may be out of sight, but I'll be close. You say the word, and I'll be at your side."

"I know." Just like he'd been at her side all night long.

They'd made love again, but slowly this time, drinking each other in, filling each other up. Neither of them wanted to admit it, but they'd made love as if they might never make love again.

An hour later, Riley wheeled her suitcase from his bedroom and parked it by the front door. Once again they'd sifted through all her items, this time looking for a key to a padlock. Carlos had seemed confident that Amy would have the key when she went to meet him, but how could he be so sure?

Amy jerked her chin toward her bag. "Do you think we should check one more time? He told me to pack a bag, so I'm assuming he hid it somewhere in my suitcase."

"We don't even know that for sure. What if he plans to take a crowbar to the lock or melt it off with a blowtorch? Maybe he ditched the key a long time ago or isn't worried that you'll bring it with you. He wants you, not the key."

"You're probably right." Amy passed her hands across her face. "Even if we found the key, there are plenty of self-storage places in San Diego with hundreds of containers. How would we ever find the right one?"

"We won't. That's why we need Carlos to lead us to the money. Once we get it and turn it over to the CIA, the cell will have no reason to go after you, and they'll have to go back to the drawing board for funding whatever it was they were planning to fund with that money."

"But that won't get you any closer to finding Jack."

"Maybe, maybe not, but I have a gut feeling Jack will be safer if we disrupt the terrorists' plans."

"We all will."

After Riley loaded her suitcase into the trunk of her car, he attached a GPS device behind her back wheel. He straightened up and brushed his hands together. "I don't think Carlos will agree to take your car, but just in case."

"You're good, Riley Hammond. You should come out of retirement."

"I'm good at taking tourists out on my dive boat, too, and it's a lot safer."

She snorted. "You don't seem like a man interested in safe."

"Will that be a problem?" He cocked his head. "Maybe *you're* not interested in safe."

The heat raced to her cheeks and she dipped her head. She'd had the same thought a hundred times, but maybe she'd finally met a man who understood the pull. She brushed her hair out of her face and smiled. "After this adventure, I'm longing for it."

"Then let's get this adventure over with." He held out his hand and she grabbed it.

He understood.

Amy jumped into her car alone, but that didn't fully describe her situation. She had the tracking device on her car and the listening device on her person. With Riley on her side, she'd never be alone.

She drove a few miles and shouted, "Can you hear me?"

Her cell phone played its ringtone immediately and she answered Riley's call.

"You don't have to shout. It's sensitive. Put the phone down and speak in a normal tone of voice, not like you're directing an ocean rescue."

Amy tossed the phone onto the seat next to her. "Is this better?"

She picked up the phone again and put it to her ear.

Riley said, "That's perfect. Now whisper sweet nothings so I can test the sound level."

Amy put the phone away from her again and whispered what she wanted to do to him once they were safely at home.

"I'd better not be hearing any of that while you're talking to Carlos."

"Hopefully, all you'll hear from me is the location of this self-storage place."

They ended the call and with it the banter, and then the enormity of her mission sucked the air from her lungs. She gripped the steering wheel, her knuckles turning white.

She'd reach the harbor soon and face Carlos, a man she once cared about. She'd have to convince him she still cared, at least long enough for Riley to track them down at the self-storage lockers and whisk her away—along with the money.

Always the money. Two sources drove Riley's motivation to steal this money out from under the terrorists' noses—to end her involvement and to disrupt any plans involving Jack. Which had the stronger pull for him?

Did it really matter? A little, persistent voice in her head argued that it did, but she ignored it. Now wasn't the time to be questioning Riley's motives.

She took the off-ramp toward the harbor and buzzed down her window to drink in the salty air. Wheeling into the parking lot, she leaned forward to study the slip numbers looking for number 815. She drove past the tourist boats, empty on this September evening in the middle of the week.

She spoke quietly as if to herself. "I'm at the harbor now. Eight-fifteen must be toward the end of the slips on the right of the parking lot entrance."

She wanted to hear Riley's confident voice in response, but she didn't dare pick up her cell phone now. Carlos could be watching her. Giving herself a brisk shake, she swung into a parking slot opposite the slips.

Would Carlos be waiting for her out in the open? She slid from the car and swung open a gate leading to the docks, the boats outlined against the sinking sun. She trudged up the ramp, spotting slip eight-fifteen with a midsize sailboat bobbing in the water.

"Carlos?" She drew back her shoulders and strode toward the boat.

A dark head popped up from the deck of the boat. His face broke out in a smile. "*Mi amor.* You made it."

"Of course."

He rose to his feet, his head jerking back and forth. "You're alone?"

"Who would I bring with me?" She spread her arms wide. "I was so happy when you called. When I thought you were dead—" She broke off and covered her face with her hands.

"*Lo siento.* There was no other way. Velasquez or the terrorists would've killed me or worse." He stretched his arms out to her. "I hoped I would regain consciousness before you came home, but when I woke up you were gone—along with my car. You know there's no wife, don't you?"

"Yes, I do. I know you pretended to be married

to keep me safe until you could come for me." Amy reached the boat and grabbed his cool hand. "Those men came after me, Carlos. I had to get away quickly and I remembered you always parked your car in the back."

He kissed her hand. "The car is nothing. We can have everything and more."

"Where is the money?"

Carlos narrowed his almost-black eyes, and Amy's pulse ticked faster. She'd have to show a little more interest in Carlos and a little less interest in his cash.

"You've come here for me and not the money, haven't you?"

Amy brushed a dark curl from his forehead. "The money is a nice surprise, but it wouldn't mean anything without you."

He nodded, his gaze shifting past her shoulder at the water. A muscle ticked in his jaw, and Amy's heart hammered. Had he seen something?

Glancing her way, he smiled but furrows remained across his brow. "I knew I could trust you, Amy. I knew a little subterfuge wouldn't scare you off. Your brother told me a lot about you. I don't think he ever imagined I'd fall in love with you, though. For him you were a means to an end—storing the drugs on the beach—but for me you became much more."

She moved her lips beneath his kiss, fighting her revulsion. Running her hand through his hair, she pulled away. "Were you planning to take the money from the deal before you met me?"

"Yes."

His eyes darted toward the water again, but Amy kept her gaze pinned to his face. She didn't want to turn around. She didn't want to give away Riley with any deed or word.

He shook his head and kissed her again. "I decided to keep that money as soon as Ethan laid out the deal to me, but once I met you my resolve deepened. I could get into my storage facility without the key, but the money would be worthless without sharing it with someone. I always wanted you and the money, Amy."

It seems as if the money and I are a package deal for everyone.

"I'm glad." She pasted a smile on her face. Her jaw ached with the effort.

She'd had enough of this reunion. Where had Carlos stashed the money? If he told her now, Riley would have a chance to get there before them. He might even have a chance to break off the lock and get the money before they even arrived.

She ground her teeth together. She didn't want to ask Carlos about the money again. She had to let him play this out his way.

"Of course now that you're here, I can use the padlock key to get into the storage locker." His sly smile spread across his face. "Do you want to know where I hid the key?"

A seagull shrieked overhead and an outboard motor hummed in the harbor while Amy held her breath. As Riley mentioned before, finding the key didn't mean a thing without the location of the self-storage facility. What if Carlos didn't tell her the location and just took her there? That would make the situation more difficult for Riley.

But Riley had a contingency plan. He had a plan for everything.

She smiled sweetly. "Where did you hide the key?"

He drew her close again, and she almost gagged on his cologne. How had she ever found that scent sexy? She preferred Riley's clean masculine smell.

Carlos ran a finger along the chain of her necklace and hooked it around his fingertip, dangling the gold heart-shaped locket at the end. "I put it in something that I knew you'd keep with you always."

Gasping, Amy closed her fingers around the keepsake from her mother. Carlos tapped her hand and she released her hold on the necklace. She glanced down as he flicked the catch with his thumbnail. A small key nestled inside the locket.

Amy choked back her fury. He'd hidden the means to his vile money in her most sacred possession? He could call her his love all he wanted. He knew nothing of love. He knew nothing of her.

She coughed and dumped the key into her hand. "Very clever. I would've never looked for it in my locket."

Riley must be smacking his forehead about now.

Carlos shrugged. "I didn't want the key on me, and I didn't want anyone to discover it on you."

"So where is this self-storage facility?" Amy flicked back her hair and slipped the key into her pocket, not meeting Carlos's steady gaze.

"Now that I have the key and you, we'll go together, and then our options are wide open. We can go to any beach in the world."

"Is it nearby? Do you want to take my car?" If Carlos didn't plan to tell her the location of the self-storage place, at least Riley could track them on the GPS.

"It's close, but we don't need to take your car."

Amy waved an arm toward the parking lot while

her knees trembled. "But my suitcase is in the trunk. It would be easy to take my car and leave it at the airport."

"You don't need your suitcase. Did you bring your passport like I asked?"

She'd brought it for show, but she had no intention of getting on a plane with Carlos and flying off to a foreign country, beach or no beach. "Yes, I have it, but I'm not going anywhere without my clothes."

His jaw tightened. "Don't be difficult now, Amy. We can get your bag from the car if you like."

She wrapped her arms around his waist and hoped Riley wasn't watching. "I can't wait to start our journey together. When I thought you were dead..."

Burying her head against his shoulder, she forced a sob from her throat.

"Shh." He smoothed her hair down her back. "It's almost over. We're almost there."

She sniffled. "I hope the facility is nearby. I can't take any more drama. Is it? Is it close?"

"It's just a few miles from here on Yale Street. I rented a unit in the very back row. It's a small place, no security guards, no security cameras."

Did you get that, Riley? She blew out a tiny, measured breath against Carlos's shirt.

"We'll be there soon, *mi amor*."

The roaring engine of a powerboat drowned out the rest of his words. Carlos tightened his grip on her and she instinctively pulled away. As she did so, she felt the small metal disc slip from her waistband. She glanced down in time to see it bounce into the water.

Carlos shouted, and it took her several seconds to realize he was yelling at the boat charging in their direction and not the listening device sinking to the bottom of the harbor.

Her eyes focused on the figures in the boat, and she screamed and staggered back. The powerboat drew up next to the slip with two men on deck pointing guns at them.

One of the men shouted, "Get down on the ground."

Amy shivered as she recognized her attacker from the Federal pen. Her knees locked and she froze.

Carlos reached under his jacket, and a zipping sound pierced the air. Carlos crumpled to his knees and fell over sideways as Amy clapped a hand over her mouth.

The men hopped off the boat, brandishing their weapons. The shooter, the man from the prison, hovered over Carlos while the other trained his weapon on Amy. "I hope you didn't kill him, Farzad. We still need information from him."

The man she'd recognized from before, Farzad, nudged Carlos's body with his foot. Carlos's blood seeped onto the gangplank, mixing with the saltwater. "He was reaching for a gun."

Farzad groped inside Carlos's jacket and pulled out the weapon tucked inside. Amy's gut rolled. What would Carlos have done to her if she hadn't willingly gotten on a plane with him?

The man aiming his gun at Amy cursed. "At least make sure he's dead this time, because it doesn't look like we're going to get anything out of him."

Farzad felt for a pulse and then shoved Carlos's body into the water with a heavy kick to his midsection. "I'll make sure this time."

Amy's tongue cleaved to the roof of her dry mouth

as she watched Carlos slip into the gently lapping water, his white face a ghastly mask before it disappeared.

Her gaze skimmed along the empty harbor, a few sailboats bobbed on the water in the distance, oblivious to the violence in their midst. Riley would be on his way to the storage facility, unaware that Carlos would never make it there alive.

Would *she?*

The man holding her at gunpoint strode toward her and jabbed his gun in her side. "Where's that man from the prison? Where's your protector?"

Good question. She lifted her shoulders. "I left him when Carlos called. I always knew Carlos wasn't dead. I just used that man for protection against you."

Fa⸺'' ⸺ eyes narrowed. "Who was he?"

An ⸺ ⸺ d spat out, "CIA."

A stream of Arabic flowed from the man holding her at gunpoint. He punctuated every exclamation by poking her in the back with a long silencer attached to his weapon.

Farzad smiled. "But that's not a problem because she knows where the money is, don't you, Amy?"

Yeah, she knew where Carlos had stashed the money, and that information had to keep her alive until she reached Riley.

She pressed her hand against the pocket where she'd slipped the key and nodded slowly, holding Farzad's dark gaze. "I know where the money is, but you need me to get it."

Chapter Fifteen

Riley parked his car around the corner from the U-Store storage facility and slipped in the front gate. Carlos had chosen a completely low-tech facility—no gate requiring a code to get in, no security guard on duty, no cameras. Perfect.

Back row. Carlos hadn't given Amy the number of the unit, but he'd told her he'd rented one in the back row.

Riley had broken out in a cold sweat when he'd lost contact with Amy, but at least Carlos had given her the location of the money before the mic went dead. No way Carlos could've discovered the small listening device tucked in Amy's clothing. It must've fallen out.

He ducked behind a large unit and scanned the ten battered units lined up along the back row. He'd wait until Carlos and Amy arrived, and then he'd plan his attack. He'd take down Carlos, rescue Amy and secure the money, interrupting the terrorists' scheme and whatever plans they had for Jack.

His muscles taut, he crouched against the storage unit, the cold from the metal seeping into his shoulders. He'd promised Amy some kind of life together after this mission. Could he deliver? April had begged him to give up his life of danger. He knew Amy never would. They suited each other. He'd felt it from the moment she'd swum up next to him to rescue two divers from the rough sea.

She'd been with him every step of the way on this perilous journey. She'd led him to the client's money, and they'd come to the end of the line together. If she could do all that for him, he could deliver on his promise of a happily-ever-after.

He glanced at his watch with a furrowed brow and flare of fear in his belly. Before the mic went out, it sounded as if Carlos had been on the verge of leaving. Why the delay? They must have retrieved Amy's suitcase from her car.

He massaged the back of his neck, his fingers digging into his flesh at the sound of a car engine. He pushed up to his feet and flattened his body against the corrugated metal of the unit.

The car stopped out of his line of vision, and he heard the doors open and then slam shut. More than two car doors? He yanked his gun out of its holster and gripped it with two hands.

He caught his breath and then ground his teeth together. Two men bracketed Amy, one holding a gun to her back—and neither one of them was Carlos.

He recognized the one with the gun as the so-called reporter at the Federal prison. He studied the other man and cursed under his breath. Ian's instincts had been correct. Farouk, the man they'd played cat and mouse with in the Middle East, was here in the flesh.

Someone must have ratted out Carlos. Maybe the Velasquez gang did it to save their own hides. Maybe Ethan had given him up before they slit his throat.

The trio started at the far end of the row, and Riley strained to hear them. Amy drew her hand out of her pocket and held up an object to the two men—the key Carlos had hidden in her locket.

Riley's throat closed and his nostrils flared. They'd kill Amy as soon as they got the money. He took aim at the head of Farouk, and then lowered his weapon once he realized Amy still had a gun shoved into her back. As much as he wanted to take down Farouk, if he shot now they'd kill her sooner rather than later.

He held his breath as Amy inserted the key into the lock of the first unit. The little group turned and shuffled toward the next unit, and Riley exhaled. Carlos had never told her which unit housed the money. They'd have to try every unit, and they wouldn't kill Amy until they had the money in their hands—just in case she was playing them.

He whispered to himself, "Keep coming this way. Keep coming this way."

They tried the second lock with no luck and then skipped the next unit as it had a combination lock on it. A bead of sweat rolled down Riley's face as he watched them approach the fourth unit.

They had come within earshot, but the three of them didn't have much to say to each other. In the quiet atmosphere, Riley's rasping breath sounded like a jet engine to his ears. They moved onto the next unit and Amy repeated the procedure. Only this time, she yelped and jumped back.

The padlock on the storage unit hung open, and Farouk and his cohort exchanged a quick glance. Riley's grip on his gun tightened as Farouk shoved Amy away from the entrance. He lifted the lock and swung open the door.

Raising his gun, Riley aimed at the man holding Amy. If he could just get her to step away from the target or drop to the ground Riley had the shot. Riley had to act quickly while Farouk was focused on the money and before he pulled out his weapon.

Farouk ducked his head into the storage unit, and adrenaline pumped through Riley's veins. He shouted, "Amy, get down."

Amy dropped to the ground as if she'd been expecting the command, and Riley squeezed the trigger. The bullet hit the man in the shoulder and he spun around with the force, dropping his weapon.

Riley charged forward while Amy kicked the gun out of the way and flung out her arms to grab the edge of the door and swing it shut. As she struggled to her knees, Farouk grabbed her around the neck, pulling her up and dragging her against his chest.

Riley loomed over the bleeding man losing consciousness on the ground and swung his weapon toward Amy's captor. The blood in his veins turned to ice when he saw the knife at her throat.

"Looks like we have a stand-off, Hammond." Farouk grinned. "I wondered if one of the Prospero team was involved. I can't say it's a pleasure to see you again, but my money's here, so if you let me leave peacefully, I'll let you have Amy."

Amy's eyes widened at the use of Riley's name.

"What if I told you reinforcements were on the way, Farouk?"

The man shrugged, skepticism etched on his face. "Then I'd kill Amy, and nobody would be happy."

Riley's hand clenched and he slid his gaze to Amy's white face. If Farouk killed Amy, it would be the last act of violence in his sorry life. "What are you going to buy with that money?"

Farouk stepped in front of the duffel bags on the floor of the unit as if to protect them. "What's your interest? I thought you just wanted to rescue the girl. You always want to rescue the girl."

He did want to rescue Amy and he wanted to rescue Jack. Could he do both? Stepping back, he massaged his temple.

"Don't let him get away with the money, Riley." The knife gleamed at Amy's neck, and her jaw tightened with resolve. Did she really believe he'd sacrifice her to stop a terrorist's plans, even if those plans involved Jack?

Riley released a measured breath. "What do you know about Jack Coburn?"

Farouk's eyes flickered but he shrugged a shoulder. "Only that he got the better of me too many times."

The blood roared in Riley's ears. *He knew something.* "He's a hostage negotiator now. He went to Afghanistan to secure the release of a captive. We don't know much more than that."

"And I know even less. I thought you were retired. What are you doing back on the job?" When his question met a stony silence from Riley, Farouk continued. "You should understand I know only a part of the plan. My job is to secure this money from the drug deal."

Riley had nothing to use as a bargaining chip but the gun in his hand. He'd get nothing from Farouk. With his muscles taut, he stepped around the unconscious man on the ground and gestured with his gun. "Take the money and leave Amy."

"No." Amy's word sliced through the air. "Don't let him take the money, Riley."

Farouk clicked his tongue. "Brave words from the daughter and the sister of criminals. I'll leave her to you once you load up the bags in the car, Hammond. Sorry I can't help you. I'm otherwise engaged."

He brought the knife closer to Amy's throat as he stepped out of the storage unit. She stumbled over the edge, and he cinched his arm around her waist. He backed up to his car and popped the trunk. "Drop your gun and get the money."

Riley's hand steadied and he narrowed his eyes.

"You make one more move with that weapon, and I'll slide this knife right across her throat. You can trust me, Hammond."

Amy gasped as Riley chucked his gun near the other man's weapon on the ground. He clambered into the unit. The warm, dry air closed around him as he hoisted the two duffel bags. Emerging into the dim light of dusk, he swallowed hard as he glanced at Farouk, his arm wrapped around Amy's body, and his knife still poised at her throat.

"Put the bags in the trunk."

Riley heaved the bags into the trunk and slammed the lid. "Now what?"

"Now Amy accompanies me in the car just for a short distance, and then I'll release her. She doesn't have to worry about us ever again. You, however… Well, I'm sure we'll meet at some point in the future."

A muscle ticked wildly in Riley's jaw. His gaze darted toward the two guns lying uselessly on the ground.

Amy gave a strangled cry as Farouk shoved her into the driver's side of the car, the knife at her back. Riley shuffled closer to his gun as he watched Amy climb over to the passenger seat. Farouk started his engine and the car lurched forward.

Riley hunched over and ran toward his gun and grabbed both weapons. He looked up in time to see the passenger door fly open and Amy tumble from the car, which never stopped. Riley scrambled for his weapon, rolled onto his stomach and took a shot at the speeding car. He got off another shot as the car careened around a corner, leaving nothing but dust in its wake.

Riley turned his attention to Amy, struggling to her knees and sobbing. He jumped to his feet and ran toward her, his heart thumping with every step.

He caught her in his arms, pulling her up and crushing her to his chest. "Are you okay? Did he hurt you?"

She dug her nails into his shoulders as she held on. "I'm fine. I just scraped my arm when I jumped from the moving car."

He ran his hand along her arm, brushing bits of dirt and gravel from her soft skin, marred with several red scratches. Now she had two injured arms. "Thank God you're okay. I would have done anything he asked while he had that knife to your throat."

"You shouldn't have let him take off with the money, Riley." She grabbed his hands and brought them to her lips. "Taking their money would have forced them to start over and given you more time to track down leads on Jack."

"I still have one lead on Jack." Riley turned his head and jerked his chin toward the wounded man on the ground.

"He's not dead?" When Farzad had crumpled to the ground, his shoulder spouting blood, Amy assumed

Riley had killed him. But one dead man had already come back to life. Why not another?

Riley tugged her hand, and she reluctantly followed him back to the gaping storage unit and the man sprawled on the ground next to it. Riley crouched beside Farzad and ripped off the bottom of the man's shirt. He bunched it up and pressed it against the wound. Were his last-ditch medical efforts too little too late?

He lightly slapped the pale face and propped up his head. "Get some water from my bag, which is around the corner from that unit."

Riley jerked his thumb over his shoulder and Amy jumped to her feet and ran toward the unit. She scooped up the black bag from the ground and plunged her hand inside for the water.

She squatted beside Riley and handed him the bottle. He twisted off the cap and splashed a few drops on Farzad's face. Farzad blinked his eyes and moaned. Riley held the bottle to his lips.

"His name is Farzad."

"You're going to be okay, Farzad. I'll call for an ambulance."

Amy cringed at the lie which brought false hope to a dying man, even though this dying man had held her at gunpoint less than fifteen minutes ago.

Farzad puckered his lips and drew the water into his mouth. Most of it ran down his chin, and he closed his eyes again. Riley dragged him to the storage unit and propped him up against the side.

"Tell me what you know about Jack Coburn."

The man squeezed his eyes and the corner of his mouth ticked up. He gasped and clutched his shoulder where fresh blood seeped from Riley's bandage.

Riley shook him and slapped his face. "Tell me what you know about Coburn."

Farzad sucked air into his mouth, and his eyes flew open. "Jack Coburn."

"That's right. Jack Coburn. What do you know about him?"

Farzad's breath rattled in his chest, and Amy knew nothing could save him now. Riley leaned in, his ear close to Farzad's moving lips.

With a last rasping breath, Farzad slumped, his head falling to the side. Riley checked his pulse and swept his palm over the dead man's eyes.

Amy dropped her head in her hands. "I'm sorry, Riley."

"Sorry? The man was a brutal killer, perhaps even involved in a plot for mass murder. There's nothing to be sorry about."

She looked up, drawing her brows over her nose. "Not that. I meant I'm sorry you didn't get anything out of him before he died."

Riley quirked an eyebrow. "Who said I didn't?"

"H-he whispered something to you at the end?"

"Yep." He pushed to his feet and pulled out his cell phone.

Amy fell back on her hands, staring up at him while a light breeze lifted his hair from his shoulders. "Well?"

Riley grinned. "He said Jack escaped."

AMY KICKED HER LEGS onto the coffee table and wrapped her hands around her sweating can of soda. She swiveled her head back and forth between Riley and his friend Ian as they discussed the implications of Farzad's dying words.

The two men didn't resemble each other in appearance. Riley's longish blond mane contrasted with Ian's dark, short-cropped hair. Riley's quick grin lit up his blue eyes, while Ian's slow smile sent a glow to his dark green eyes.

But energy emanated from both men's finely tuned and trained bodies. Their jobs since retiring from Prospero—Riley's running a dive boat and Ian's leading mountain climbing expeditions—both contained an element of adventure and danger. But the very air around them crackled with intensity as they exchanged ideas about Jack's situation.

Ian stretched and rubbed his knuckles across his head. "I had a feeling Farouk and his gang were involved, but the question remains. What exactly did Jack escape from?"

"And if he escaped—" Riley snapped his fingers "—he's not some kind of traitor."

"Then where is he? If your guy was telling the truth about Jack, why hasn't he contacted anyone?"

Riley shook his head. "I don't know. Follow the money. It's out of our hands now, but it will soon be in somebody else's. We need to pick up chatter and see where we're at."

Sipping her soda, Amy drew her brows together. "Where do you guys get this chatter anyway?"

"Should we tell her?" Riley raised his brows up and down.

Ian winked. "I don't know. It's top secret."

"After what I've been through? I should be an honorary member of Prospero."

Riley dropped on the couch next to her and squeezed her knee. "It's no mystery. We get chatter through tapped phones, hacked email accounts, undercover agents on the ground and imprisoned terrorists looking to make deals. We use any and all sources."

"We'll hear something soon about this money." Ian rose from his chair and crushed his empty beer can. "Something will give. Information about a deal this big will slip through somewhere. And I'll be ready."

"*You'll* be ready? What about me? What about Buzz?"

"Buzz, maybe, but you've done your part."

Riley threaded his fingers through Amy's and pulled her up with him. "Unless the hunt takes us back to the ocean. Then I'm your man."

Amy slipped her arm around his waist. "You're *my* man."

Ian laughed. "And with those well-chosen words, I'm off. Take a break, Riley. We'll keep you posted."

"If Jack's in any danger, any danger at all, come and get me."

Ian pulled Amy from Riley's arms and kissed her on the cheek. "Keep this guy out of trouble." Then he flashed a thumbs-up sign to Riley and left.

Riley tipped Ian's crushed beer can, which he'd left on the countertop, and sent it rocking back and forth. "If he calls, I have to go, Amy."

"I know that." She wound her arms around his neck.

He kissed her mouth and she melted against him.

"And when the danger ends? When we find Jack?" He studied her face, but she had nothing to hide.

"Even if you never go on another mission for as long as you live, you're all I need, Riley."

Running his hands through her hair, he deepened the kiss. "I need you, too, Amy. But as long as one of my brothers in arms is in trouble, I'll go through hell and back to help him."

"I wouldn't have it any other way, Riley Hammond. In fact, I'm counting on it."

Epilogue

He rolled to his side and jerked back, inches from a twenty-five foot drop. He worked his jaw, grit and sand grinding between his teeth. Dragging himself up to a sitting position, he leaned against the rough surface of a flat rock. His lungs demanded air as he surveyed the mountainous terrain through squinted eyes. A village, or at least a collection of ramshackle buildings, lay in a valley gorge between two peaks.

His breathing eased and with each deep breath, all the pains in his body came roaring to life. Gasping, he gingerly probed his rib cage. A bruised or broken rib howled in protest at the intrusion.

He wiped a hand across his face and studied the streaks of blood and dirt on his palm. He ran his tongue around his lips, wincing at the pain in one tender spot, but tasting no blood. One side of his face felt scorched, and he dabbed his fingers along his right cheekbone, following the paths of several scratches across his face.

He wove his fingers through tangled hair, matted with a sticky substance—must be more blood. His fingertips traced around a huge knot on the back of his head. The blood had come from another cut. There was no broken skin across the solid lump.

Stretching out one arm and then the other, he wiggled his fingers. Everything seemed to be in working—if painful—order. He hoisted to his haunches. His bones ached but they moved and supported his body.

A bird screeched overhead and he twisted around, catching a glimpse of the ledge above him. He could climb to the precipice, or he could scramble down the mountainside to the little village.

What kind of reception awaited him there?

He cleared his throat and shaded his eyes against the rising sun, a yellow egg yolk spreading in the morning sky. He crawled to the edge of his own private ledge, the ledge that probably saved his life.

Leaning forward, he spotted a rough trail meandering down the side of the mountain. If he could clamber down the boulders that tumbled toward that pathway, he could follow it into the village.

Surely, someone would offer help—food, some simple first aid for his injuries. Surely, someone could tell him where he was.

Maybe someone could even tell him who he was.

* * * * *

Carol Ericson's BROTHERS IN ARMS *miniseries
continues next month with Ian Dempsey's story,
MOUNTAIN RANGER RECON.
Look for it wherever Harlequin Intrigue
books are sold!*

Harlequin®

INTRIGUE®

COMING NEXT MONTH

Available April 12, 2011

#1269 GI COWBOY
Daddy Corps
Delores Fossen

#1270 MISSING
Colby Agency: The New Equalizers
Debra Webb

#1271 WATERFORD POINT
Shivers
Alana Matthews

#1272 HITCHED AND HUNTED
Cooper Justice: Cold Case Investigation
Paula Graves

#1273 MOUNTAIN RANGER RECON
Brothers in Arms
Carol Ericson

#1274 BULLETPROOF HEARTS
Kay Thomas

HiCNM0311

REQUEST YOUR FREE BOOKS!
2 FREE NOVELS PLUS 2 FREE GIFTS!

◆ Harlequin®

INTRIGUE®

BREATHTAKING ROMANTIC SUSPENSE

*Selene wanted nothing to do with the father of her son,
Alex; but Aristedes had other plans...that included them.*

*Read on for an sneak peek from
THE SARANTOS SECRET BABY by Olivia Gates,
available April 2011, only from Harlequin Desire.*

"You were right to turn my marriage offer down," Aristedes said.

And Selene found her voice at last, found the words that
would not betray the blow he'd dealt her. "Thanks for letting me know. You didn't have to come all the way here,
though. You could have just let it go. I left yesterday with
the understanding that this case is closed."

Before the hot needles behind her eyes could dissolve
into an unforgivable display of stupidity and weakness, she
began to close the door.

The door stopped against an immovable object. His flat palm.

"I can't accept that." His voice was low, leashed.

What did her tormentor mean now? Was he ending one
game only to start another?

She raised eyes as bruised as her self-respect to his,
found nothing there but solemnity and determination.

Before she could voice her confusion, he elaborated. "I
never let anything go unless I'm certain it's unworkable. I
realize I made you an unworkable offer, and that's why I'm
withdrawing it. I'm here to offer something else. A work-
ability study."

She leaned against the door, thankful for its support and
partial shield. "Your son and I are not a business venture
you can test for feasibility."

His gaze grew deeper, made her feel as if he was trying
to delve into her mind, take control of it. "It's actually the

other way around. I'm the one who would be tested."

She shook her head. "Why bother? I know—and *you* know—you're not workable. Not with me."

His spectacular eyebrows lowered over eyes she felt were emitting silver hypnosis. "You're right again. Neither you nor I have any reason to believe that isn't the truth. The only truth. It might be best for both you and Alex to never hear from me again, to forget I exist. But then again, maybe not. I'm only asking for the chance for both of us to find out for certain. You believe I'm unworkable in any personal relationship. I've lived my life based on that belief about myself. I never really had reason to question it. But I have one now. In fact, I have two."

Find out what happens in
THE SARANTOS SECRET BABY by Olivia Gates,
available April 2011, only from Harlequin Desire.

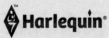

Harlequin® *Blaze*™
red-hot reads

Sunny, sensual Hawaiian spring break…again!

Three best girlfriends are recapturing an amazing spring-break vacation they had a decade ago.

First on the beach is former attorney and all-around good girl Mia Butterfield. Meeting up with her boyfriend of old is a bust, so she's shocked when her hero turns out to be someone she'd never have expected…

Find out who it is in
SECOND TIME LUCKY
by acclaimed author
Debbi Rawlins

Available from Harlequin Blaze® April 2011

Part of the sensual miniseries,
Spring Break

Part 2: Delicious Do-Over (May)

A *Romance* FOR EVERY MOOD™

www.eHarlequin.com